"WHO'S THIS LO____ ___ ___ ASKED.

They were nearing the theater exit when Andrea heard the question. But at that moment, a woman in a hurry forced her way between them, and Andy's mumbled reply was lost.

"Are you hungry?" he asked.

"Not anymore, Tom. As a matter of fact, I feel very drained . . . I have some thinking to do." That was an understatement! Andy was in turmoil. She was engaged to Lowell, yet she could still feel the warmth of Tom's hand holding hers and see his dark, Gypsy eyes.

"Well, let me see you home."

She agreed, and he accompanied Andy to her apartment entrance. But when he bent down to kiss her, she stepped back, gently touched his cheek and said, "Thanks, Tom."

Despite his expression of puzzled yearning, she firmly closed the door. "Please, please leave," she prayed softly, "before I make a fool of myself—if I haven't already." Finally, she heard his reluctant steps turn to go.

In her apartment she flopped across the bed, groaning in frustration and confusion. Her eyes fell on the tiny box that held an immense diamond engagement ring. Tomorrow she would become officially engaged to Lowell Curtis. By next week, all of Boston will know it, she thought with a groan . . . and Tom will know it. "Andy Ferguson," she said aloud, "what are you going to do?"

The BRIDE AND GROOM series:

I Do, I Don't
Just Family and Friends
Country Bride
The Best Man

The Best Man
Robin St. Joan

LYNX BOOKS
New York

BRIDE AND GROOM: THE BEST MAN

ISBN: 1-55802-050-0

First Printing/April 1989

This is a work of fiction. Names, characters, places, and incidents are either the product of the author's imagination or are used fictitiously. Any resemblance to actual events, locales, or persons, living or dead, is entirely coincidental.

Copyright © 1989 by the Jeffrey Weiss Group, Inc.
All rights reserved. No part of this book may be reproduced or transmitted in any form or by any means electronic or mechanical, including by photocopying, by recording, or by any information storage and retrieval system, without the express written permission of the Publisher, except where permitted by law. For information, contact Lynx Communications, Inc.

This book is published by Lynx Books, a division of Lynx Communications, Inc., 41 Madison Avenue, New York, New York, 10010. The name "Lynx" and the logo consisting of a stylized head of a lynx are trademarks of Lynx Communications, Inc.

Printed in the United States of America

0 9 8 7 6 5 4 3 2 1

To Frank

Bride and Groom

ONE

Andy Ferguson slammed the door of her old VW Rabbit and dashed toward the changing rooms of the Cambridge Tennis Club. She caught a glimpse of spring sunshine dimpling the Charles River. She was late, as usual, and Lowell was bound to be on time.

Lowell Curtis had asked her to marry him less than a week after their first meeting, if being pulled out of the snow could be called a meeting....

She had gone to Stowe for a week of good Vermont skiing, and after a few runs down the intermediate slopes, she'd decided to try a tough one, the Goat. Halfway down and going much too fast for someone out of practice, she hit a mogul and found herself sprawled in the snow, with a throbbing ankle. Luckily, Lowell had seen her fall and came to her aid. A stretcher was quickly summoned to get her to the lodge. There, after a few shaky moments of testing the ankle, she decided it wasn't broken, only badly sprained.

"Let me introduce myself," he said, smiling. "Lowell Curtis at your service and you are. . . ?"

"Andy, uh, Andrea Ferguson," she stammered, recognizing his name.

Lowell Curtis was the successful, upper-crust son of a wealthy Boston banker. His picture had appeared more than once in her paper, the *Boston Tribune*. In one, he was showing a clutch of Japanese businessmen the State House, in another, accepting the Falk Tennis Trophy at Longwood. He appeared so much handsomer than his photos, she thought, noting the fine blond hair—thick on top and clean-cut on the sides—the mischievous blue eyes, the fine, clear lines of his face. He certainly is Prince Charming, Andy told herself. Too bad I'm not a Princess.

At twenty-six, she was tall and slim, but as a child, she'd been an ugly duckling, and a tomboy—taller than the boys in her class, a tough competitor in sports, and captain of the basketball team. In late high school and college, things began to change. Her long, muscular body began to develop interesting curves. Boys began to notice her and treat her differently. Her good bones were highlighted by a healthy glow and the famous Andy grin. She preferred the easy companionship of men, but she liked being a woman among them.

"Come on," he said. "We'll order you a hot toddy and then you'll do me the honor of dining with me at Chez Bernice."

They drove about twenty miles south of Stowe and found the restaurant half-full, candlelit, and gastronomically superb.

"They don't rush things here," he said over his martini. "That'll give me time to find out all about my snow maiden." A little hesitant at first, Andy began to talk about her work. He laughed.

"So you're the famous Andy, uh, Andrea Ferguson, terror of bureaucracy. Good thing for me I met you before you uncovered all my guilty secrets."

She spoke briefly about her father. His sudden death from a stroke four years earlier still had the power to raise tears at the least expected moments. She told Lowell of how much she loved her father's ranch, the Blue Ridge, which he'd left to her. The big, ungainly house, barn, and some outbuildings weren't much to look at, but the surrounding sixty acres were part of what her father called "the prettiest land in God's country"—high in the Colorado Rockies. The ranch still held too many memories, she explained, which was why she hadn't been back.

She described her mother's triumphant return to Boston. Shortly after Ben's stroke, Grace Ferguson's uncle had left her a healthy legacy. She had insisted they leave Denver, so that at least Amy, her younger daughter, could have the privileges only the East could offer. And Grace thought it was time for Andrea to widen her opportunities, too. Andy, still stunned, had reluctantly agreed.

"My sister is very pretty and smart, too," she explained to Lowell. "But I swear she'd rather go dancing seven times a week than think about getting a real job. She's done some local TV spots, but she's too short to model—I'm the giraffe in the family—but she does have a real feeling for design, for interior decoration. She thinks my place looks like the motel room in *Psycho*. She's always threatening to jazz it up. But then Mom was always going on about antiques and English furniture. I guess Mom's talk really rubbed off on her."

Andy blushed, embarrassed that she may have been talking too much about herself. In the pause that followed, she suddenly thought how excited her mother and sister would be if they could see her now, dining with Lowell Curtis, the well-known international banker and sportsman. Wow! For her part, she found him charming, but was wary of all his glamour. In the past, she'd had a couple of semi-serious relationships: a boy in graduate school and an attractive rancher in Denver who had turned out to be married. That one had left her a bit scorched. Her father's death, the subsequent move East, and her busy job had left little time for dating, much less romance.

She wondered what a jet-setter like Lowell saw in her. One of her best-honed journalistic tools was an ability to really listen. This time it was no hardship. He was fascinating. After a brief discussion with the waiter about *langouste*, which turned out to be lobster, he asked for a wine list and engaged in a lively discussion that produced a bottle of Château Gris. She noted the label after sipping it and had to curtail her urge to reach for the reporter's notebook in her purse. For the first time she felt the gaps in her education. Andy's mother knew some French and insisted that Amy study it. Andy had elected Spanish instead, which she spoke haltingly. Weren't there a lot more Hispanics in Colorado and even Boston than French people? Now she briefly regretted her mother's warnings about neglecting more refined studies: music, art, history, poetry. She smiled, remembering her father's delight in such elegant verses as "The Day Larry Got Stretched."

"I'm no expert, but you could pass for French with that accent. How did you manage that?" Lowell ordered *deux calvados* and leaned forward with a smile.

"I can't take credit for that. I was shipped off to Switzerland, a simple Boston lad, to be transformed into a cosmopolitan dandy at Le Rosey. Mother's brother Binky went there and though he turned out rather a black sheep—too much booze, no ambition—he does cut a fine figure at parties. He speaks French and Italian, knows everyone from the Ali Khan to Prince Ranier, squires all the wealthy widows in town. Mother wanted me to have his advantages, and Dad knew the contacts would be great if I went into the firm. The place was all right, I guess, especially since it went co-ed after Binky's time. I made excellent contacts, mostly with the wrong sex." He laughed wryly and looked directly into her eyes. She looked away slightly. "You know, Andrea, I've met a lot of women, but none quite like you."

"It's my exotic Colorado charm; a little provincial, I'm afraid, but loyal and honest and willing to learn."

Was he giving her a line suddenly? Was she giving one back?

"I guess that sounded pretty trite, but it's true," Lowell said. "We're really talking, not trying to one-up each other with the usual Boston gossip. It's so boring sometimes. I like the way you talk, your accent, and the way you listen as if you're really interested."

"Well, I am interested. This is all new to me. You talk a good game, Mr. Curtis. And you know so much about"—she waved her arm, almost upsetting her wineglass—"well, the world. Tell me about those wrong contacts."

"You don't miss a thing, do you? Well it was mostly for kicks, you know, nothing too serious. Once I was invited along with Freddi Orsini and his family to a weekend party in Scotland, one of those god-awful castles they insist on maintaining. Well, there was this wild bunch of tall stones near the entrance. I asked McKuan what they were and he said they were some kind of pagan altar. Said his ancestors bashed out their enemies' brains on them—ha, ha—and all that. We had roast pig and venison cooked on a spit for supper. He kept pouring drinks until he passed out at the table, and we were forced to leave the fire and go off to our freezing little cells that served as our bedrooms. I couldn't sleep, of course.

"About two-thirty, Freddi's sister—I'd met her once at school when she was only a kid—came into my room, shivering, begging me to hold her for just a little while, just to get warm. Well, I could hardly refuse a lady, a contessa at that, and it made sense in a way. It got a lot warmer. Anyway, I thought I'd better get her back before her honor was sullied, but we couldn't find her room. And who do we run into but Freddi, trying to find the loo. It would have been pistols at dawn, but she swore our innocence and finally calmed him down. They left before breakfast."

He followed this with the story of the time he narrowly escaped being trapped into a shotgun wedding with a Greek heiress who had lured him into her suite on the family yacht. After much champagne, she suddenly shucked off her caftan, all she was wearing, and leaped on him like a tiger. When he'd shown signs of demurring, she had rung for her maid, who was willing to swear that Lowell was the aggressor.

"I don't remember quite how I got out of that one."

He laughed at Andy's expression of bewilderment. "Come on, Andrea. All's fair in love and business. That's how she felt, that if she couldn't have me, she'd sue. A clever bunch, those Greeks. Remember the Trojan horse?"

She remembered. One of her childhood heroes was Odysseus, her dad's favorite. Suddenly she felt terribly sleepy. Her ankle had begun to throb in spite of her efforts to keep it raised. He noticed at once and ordered the check. It was more than she cared to think about. She was a trifle surprised at the relatively small tip but was sure Lowell knew a lot more than she did on that subject. They drove back quietly in the warmth of his Peugeot—blue to match his eyes, she thought drowsily.

"I've really enjoyed this evening," he said as they entered the lodge. She smiled her pleasure and allowed him to help her up the stairs to her room. A quick kiss on the cheek, a long look in her eyes, and he was gone. She limped into the bathroom and was rather amused by the soppy expression in her usually cool eyes. Yes, he was something else. She liked him a lot—a lovely evening. She took an aspirin to quiet her ankle and fell asleep thinking about Switzerland and Scotland and the Greek Isles, all those wonderful places she had never seen.

She woke up late the next day and was immediately aware of a howling wind. She limped quickly to the window, pulled the blind, and was startled to see wildly blowing snow. The storm had struck full force, and all the slopes would be impossible, she thought, hearing a knock at the door.

"Oh, hold on a minute" she yelled and scurried into a yellow terry-cloth wrapper. She opened the door to behold a room-service waiter holding a tray laden with bacon, eggs, croissants, coffee, and jams. He entered to set up the lovely meal and a moment later was followed by the smiling presence of Lowell Curtis, wearing the same handsome blue blazer and lazy smile. He handed her a yellow rose.

"Breakfast was nothing. They were very sympathetic about my invalid friend. But I almost ditched the car finding this."

"Oh, my gosh, how lovely. Oh, Lowell, what a crazy, sweet thing to do. The roads must be awful. How did you even get here?"

"Okay. I cannot tell a lie. Last night, when I started home, I heard the forecast on the radio. The thought of being holed up in that big, lonely chalet for God knows how long made me turn around and head straight back here. Thank God they had a room, not more than a glorified broom closet with a bed and shower. Anyway, let's eat. Then we'll plan the day. You are in luck, my lady. There's no skiing, so I'm all yours. By the way, how's your backgammon game?"

"My what? Oh, backgammon. I'm afraid that wasn't in my curriculum, but I'll stake the Ferguson fortune on a little three-card monte or blackjack."

Lowell shook his head in mock horror.

"None of your vulgar cowpoke games today. I'll teach you to play. You'll love it."

After breakfast Lowell excused himself, and Andy dressed, wishing she had paid a little more attention to her packing. But she hadn't really counted on meeting anyone special. Some minutes later, wearing jeans and an old Fair Isle sweater, she eased herself downstairs to find Lowell waiting.

"You look great, love that jersey. I got us a table

in the room off the bar. They'll need it later for a big party. It seems that two of the guests are getting married if they can find the church in this storm. This place usually caters to singles, but they met here last year. We're all invited to the reception."

"Oh, gosh, Lowell, I'm afraid I didn't bring anything fancy. You've seen my best blouse already."

"What about me? I may be stuck in this shirt for days, but I found one of those places that sell everything, and got a razor and more important—*voilà!*"

He produced a tiny traveling backgammon set, and when they were comfortable, he began to explain the rules as simply as possible.

"Actually, there's nothing to it until you begin to see the patterns and the traps. You'll catch on. We won't play for money."

"Well, thanks a lot. I can barely afford this place as it is." She learned quickly despite a tendency to take risks, and pounced on his pieces with delight.

"Careful, Andrea. You're leaving your board wide open. You want to try to fill it across. Then, when you get me, I'll be stuck."

"Oh, that's no fun. Is it my turn?"

She threw double fives. Lowell sighed. Double threes. Lowell frowned. She shook the die with abandon. Double sixes. Her eyes gleamed with predatory delight as she drove her men home.

"You are so damn lucky, Andrea. If this were for money I'd be in hock up to my knees. But remember, I'll get you in the end." She won that game and Lowell calmly trounced her in the next three.

"How the heck did you do that? I was way ahead!"

"Andrea, you—God you're fun to play with," Lowell said, laughing. "You get so excited, but you're too impulsive. See, I quietly filled my board across so when I caught you, you couldn't get in, and all your turns were wasted. It's okay. You'll be a champ in no time. But you've got to be more careful. Hold on. I'll get us a couple of Beck's."

Got to be more careful ... more careful. The words echoed in her mind, calling up her the memory of her father. *Take it easy, Andy, and you'll get there.* He had always kidded her out of the blues, told her he knew she would make it, but cautioned her always to take the time to learn her craft. His death still left her feeling helpless and unanchored. At night she would dream of her father and wake shouting, "Daddy, where are you? Daddy, help me." Then she'd feel the familiar pain—and anger. Why couldn't he have stayed around for her? Why? Remorse always followed. He was still her beloved Daddy, her champion and her conscience.

She stared out at the churning snow and recalled the day Ben and she had been caught in a fluke September blizzard at the ranch. They had gone up alone one weekend to ride and deliver the horses to their winter quarters with a farmer in the valley. Ben sensed a change in the weather the first night and elected to ride down the mountain first thing in the morning. The horses were safely installed at Kluger's farm and they were halfway home when huge, wet flakes began to block out the sky.

"Looks bad," Ben murmured in a way Andy knew meant danger.

"All right now, take a bead on that stand of aspens up there and go like hell. If we get there soon enough, we'll still be able to see the house."

They ran, stumbled, and climbed, forgetting the dirt road that was fast disappearing, and made it just in time to get a directional fix on the dark green of the porch and the old flagpole. By the time they arrived, panting and soaked, they could hardly get the door open.

"Andy honey," her father sighed, letting his real concern show, "the state of Colorado just almost lost two of its dumbest geniuses—one, anyway. Maybe we should have stayed at Kluger's."

They staggered inside, stomping and shaking snow off like wet horses. Thank God he had thought to bring in a supply of wood when they arrived. There were canned goods galore so hunger was no immediate problem. But to be snowed in at nearly nine thousand feet could be rough. They built the fire Indian style as her father called it, the logs shaped like a low tepee to allow lots of air through. Ben reminisced about finding the ranch for sale while doing research on mining lore.

"If it hadn't been for the book. . ."

The little weekly paper he had started had failed to make a go of it so he'd sold it and taken off six months to write a book on Western scouts. *Rocky*

Mountain Blazes was published and sold well enough to enable him to buy the ranch—"a steal," he said—and to start his own small publishing house, the Timberline Press. His writing success was never repeated, but he continued to print the work of local writers, cowboy poetry, and anything he considered worthwhile without giving too much thought to profits. Grace often complained that the ranch was eating up everything extra, but she and Amy enjoyed it, too, in midsummer, and she knew better than to suggest he give it up.

"I keep thinking we ought to buy those lower acres," he said. "If we don't, the damned mining syndicate will, and God knows how they'll leave it."

Andy had won a scholarship to the Columbia School of Journalism for a series she had submitted to the *Denver Courier* about the latest stripmining ravages. Her chief concerns were with the families who had been moved out and the destruction of the mountains.

Now and then she would glance out the window, but if anything, the snow and wind had joined forces more strongly to build great dunes against the northeast side of the house. After a supper of corned-beef hash and buttered beans, her father sat back, contented.

"I tell you what, kid. Let's have a couple of Scotches, double for me, and we'll have a go at 'The Road to Mandelay.' You take the harmony. That should warm us up."

Finally they filled hot-water bottles, piled on the

quilts, and slept. Next morning the snow was clear up against the first-floor windows.

"We'll have to wait, Andy. There's more coming." Ben was worried. But on the following day, Monday, the sky was clear. Andy insisted on crawling out the least difficult window over the porch. After squirming around like a seal, she was forced to slide back.

"It's at least five feet out there, Daddy. Maybe if we could get to the barn, we could ski down to Kluger's place."

"Yeah, darling, and how do we get to the barn?" They cooked a big feed of flapjacks and strong coffee while Ben scratched his head in concentration. "Snow shoes. That's the ticket. Think, Andy. What can we use to make 'em?"

She rushed around, flinging open cupboards, seizing rope and heavy tape. An old washboard presented itself, then a small grill and a dog-eared world atlas. Finally they took four bed slats from upstairs. Dressed in heavy parkas with a shovel and a knife, matches and chocolate for emergencies, they shimmied out and somehow taped and tied their boots to the heavy boards.

"Hell, Andy, we could ski down on those." But it wasn't that easy. First the snow had to be stomped down, but then the boards would hit a loose spot and send them sprawling. A good half hour later they reached the barn, dug a space around the big door, and shouldered it open. With much relief they donned their skis, grabbed their poles, and started the long descent down the mountain. The Klugers were delighted to see them. Even old, surly Otto Kluger cracked a smile.

"We wondered when you'd get here. Should've known you city folks would get yourselves stuck. I reckon the plough'll be out by afternoon. Jeth can take you to the bus stop in the Jeep. Denver bus should make it to Parshall around five."

That was the longest spiel they'd ever heard from Otto. After that, he lit his pipe and let Elsie and the boys take over. The youngest, Fritz, had developed a heavy crush on Andy the summer before. He kept offering her his Camels, and when she accepted he would make a big show of lighting a kitchen match with his thumb. They ate Elsie's stew and shared Ben's chocolate. The plow finally came and the bus was only two hours late. Andy slept blissfully on Ben's shoulder for the three bumpy hours to Denver. That was Monday. On Thursday the call came from Ben's office: "He just grabbed his chest, swore, and went down. The ambulance is coming, but I'm worried." Andy called a taxi—the car was still snowbound—and told Grace and Amy to stop crying until they knew the worst. But Andy already knew. The damn ranch had killed him—and the snow. She shouldn't have let him shovel. They should have waited. Damn him. How could he do this to her? Oh, Daddy, she thought. Oh God let him live, let him live. She clenched her teeth and prayed. But he was already gone.

At the funeral Andy stood stonily while the others wept. As they slowly eased themselves, she grew more and more closed. All her tears were in her heart and head, threatening to drown her from inside....

"Andrea—hey, Andrea. For a second I thought I'd lost you. Why so pale and wan, fair lady?"

She turned, feeling dislocated, then smiled.

"I'm sorry, Lowell. I was just thinking about a storm out in Colorado."

"Tell me about it. I want to know all about you. You know that." She hesitated a moment, then switched the conversation to skiing. What was it like in Switzerland? He described the various hazards of the Vasserngnat as compared to Vispille and Egglie, the danger of avalanches. She confessed that she was out of practice—that was obvious from her injury—but four years ago she had done Ajax Mountain in Aspen with the best, the best being Ben.

"Ajax is good," agreed Lowell, the connoisseur, "but Taos is even better. You take the lift up as far as it goes. Then a helicopter gets you to the top, and down you go in fine powder. No glare ice. No moguls." They finally ordered lunch with bloody marys.

"After all, it's a holiday from a holiday," he laughed. "How's the pretty ankle? We might try the run on Madonna when you're all better."

That night they attended that wedding reception for the singles who'd met here not long ago. They drank toast after toast of champagne. Lowell said it was rank poison and threatened to order their own bottle of Dom Perignon, but Andy refused.

"You're already sweeping me off my feet. You want me to lose them completely?"

"You bet I do. Completely. Come on. Let's dance. Oh hell, I forgot the old ankle. Forgive me, Andrea. We'll just sit here like an old married couple."

"No, Lowell, go ahead and dance. To tell you the truth, I'm not that good at it, and I hate saying I'm sorry all the time. Now if Amy were here—"

"I'm not interested in Amy. It's her big sister that turns me on. Tell you what. Let's slip into the lounge. They'll all be at the party, and we can sit by the fire and relax. Come on, Andrea." The resonance of her name hung in the air as Lowell took off for the bar. But Andrea wasn't her name, really. Oh, maybe legally, but she had always been Andy to herself and those around her. She should have made that clear. Or was she in some way playing a part or even playfully wishing to change into someone a little more feminine, a little more sophisticated? Could be. Andy was Ben's name for her. He had once admitted that he'd always wanted a boy—a boy he could share his dreams with, his love of the mountains, skiing, horses, Western lore. A son would have been named Andrew, after Ben's father. She recalled her father's words. . . .

"When you came along, I forgot all about wanting a boy. We called you Andrea but you were always Andy to me. . . . Your mother had a hard time after you were born. Some kind of depression. We couldn't afford a nurse then so I got to do a lot of feeding and burping and even diaper changing. Damn right, I did. And the first time you gave me that big Andy grin I was all yours. Good thing you didn't know it then. I used to read you *Treasure Island.* Remember? Andykins, you were all the boys and girls I ever wanted. I think Mother was a little jealous for a while, but then Amy came along and they've always been like two peas—like us, I guess, so it worked out okay."

"Here you are, love," said Lowell, handing her a brandy. He was so good-looking. She smiled up and held out her hand to accept.

Andy Ferguson, chided a sterner voice from within, you've had more booze in the last two days than in the last two months.

So? replied the newly hatched butterfly. It's time you started having some fun, feeling like a woman, for a change. Besides, how can you resist him? There was no reply. They drank, talked, and laughed together until the partygoers began drifting in.

'Andrea," Lowell murmurred. "Beautiful name, like its owner. Let's get you upstairs and tomorrow we might try Madonna. It's an easy run down. We'll take it slow and be back for dinner. If the ankle acts up we can stop over."

The next day, however, was dark and foggy. Her ankle ached a little. She and Lowell spent the day lazily, reading, playing cards and backgammon, and talking until late over hot-buttered rum.

The next day was perfect. The snow lay pure and gleaming. She stepped gingerly out of bed and, sure enough, the ankle held. The more she walked, the better it felt. She dressed and was on her way to seek out Lowell's broom closet when she spotted him near the dining room, all smiles.

"Terrific. I was sure you'd be okay. Dr. Curtis declares the patient cured and prescribes food and exercise." They started off for the slopes in the company of two other young couples.

"You know the Kennedys love Madonna," said one of the young men to Lowell as they waited for the lift. "I ran into Kathleen last year. I guess she's too busy now with the elections coming up."

Lowell smiled but didn't reply. Andy wondered what connection, if any, the Curtis and Kennedy clans might have. Now was not the time to probe. They floated up Mount Mansfield on the lift and skied down at a leisurely pace, making wide circles. The snow was fine, still powder enough. Although he insisted she take it easy, he didn't want to lose sight of the others altogether.

"We don't want them calling the ski patrol, letting everyone know where we are. I've already phoned the bank and told them I'd be taking some extra time. I'm afraid I exaggerated the driving hazards."

"I've still got until Monday," she said. "Pete Steiner, my boss—I told you about him—practically ordered me out of the office. This is my first real vacation since I started there. He's got two of the guys covering the Sorley-Bradford campaign. I kept telling him I was right for it. I mean I've met Sorley. Liked his wife and kids. I think I could do an original profile on him for 'Painting the Town.' That's my feature column, remember? We're supporting Bradford, of course."

Lowell gave her an odd look and started to say something, but changed his mind.

"Come on now. No shop talk, we'd better try to

catch up." By the time they'd crossed the lake and started down the last slope, she began to feel her ankle again. It was definitely throbbing. Lowell noticed her look of concentration and the slight drag on her left ski.

"My fault," he said with concern. "Don't tell me you're fine, because I know it hurts. Now look, there's no need to make it back this afternoon. I can rent a Jeep, and we can spend the night at Jason's chalet. It's only a couple of miles, and if I don't change my clothes soon, I'll be getting moldy and you won't want to get near me."

For the briefest moment, Andy wondered if Lowell had planned this in advance, then dismissed the notion as uncharitable. After all, she had agreed to come.

"That sounds lovely. Is there food?"

"Oh sure, he keeps the place stocked all winter. We can defrost in the microwave. I brought some lettuce and wine. This will give me a chance to show off my culinary brilliance. If the market ever taps out, I can always get a job as a cook."

She tried to imagine Lowell behind the stove at some greasy-spoon. No way—maybe at Joseph's in Boston giving orders and tasting things. No, not likely. Lowell married to the little Orsini girl, tossing a salad in their, what do you call it, palazzo, ummm. Lowell concocting the perfect omelet in her kitchenette on Linnean Street. She smiled, embarrassed, glad he couldn't read thoughts.

TWO

THE CHALET WAS a little chilly, but big white furry rugs covered the huge living room floor and a large couch was situated near a working fireplace at right angles to the picture window. Lowell instructed Andy to check out the freezer while he adjusted the thermostat and thrust two cocktail glasses into the tiny bar refrigerator. He then carefully poured a generous allowance of Tanqueray gin and a whiff of vermouth into a pitcher for the perfect martini. An ice maker merrily chunked its squares into the mixture as Lowell stirred until the required coldness matched the new, properly frosted glasses.

"Oh my gosh, Lowell, he must have a whole cow in that freezer; chickens, everything. But it's all frozen solid. Oh, martinis—well, great."

Her father had always warned her against guys bearing gins. "Creeps up on you," he'd say, "and the next thing you know, you're dancing on the table and telling the piano player he's better than Hoagy Carmichael." She'd told him she wasn't a dancer, and anyway she'd never heard of Hoagy Whatshisname. She sipped the chilled drink and decided it wasn't bad. In fact, it was kind of nice. Yes, a perfect scene—all she needed was a cigarette. She pushed the sudden longing away. After Ben's death, she'd gone up to two packs a day. It was Pete Steiner who had shamed her into quitting after she fell asleep at her desk and nearly set the whole office on fire. Six months now. Lowell raised his glass and looked at her a moment before saying, "To us! I mean that, Andrea. I like 'us' a whole lot. I haven't felt so relaxed with anyone in years. No, that's too negative—so alive with anyone. You make me like myself almost as much as I like you."

"That's nice. And you make me feel different— I'm starting to know a new me, thanks to you. I like it. It's exciting. You're always keeping me a little off balance, and it makes me feel a bit dizzy, like this drink."

She laughed and stretched her arms above her head as if she were reaching up for something or falling.

"We could have a fire," he said, "though it's warm enough without."

"Oh yes. Let's have a fire anyway. I love fires. Fire and snow. Let's not pull the curtains. It's so beautiful out there. I miss the stars, living in Boston. After supper, we can look at them."

He leaned over and slowly kissed her mouth. Her head felt liquid and light. The shadowy inner voice from her old self seemed to whisper, Andy, you're in foreign waters now. You've known this guy less than three days and you're swimming into the big waves without looking back. Yes, said the newly emerging princess voice, and having the time of my life. There was no answer. She made the fire with birch logs that had been piled in an elegant iron holder while Lowell unfroze some beef medallions in the microwave and set potatoes in the oven to bake. He chopped, measured, and tasted. When she offered to help, he shooed her away and said she could do the dishes.

"You mean put them in the machine?"

"Well, there's a pan or two that might need scrubbing."

"Okay, boss. Long as I don't have to think. I don't think I could at this point."

The beef was light and delicious with a béarnaise sauce, the potatoes hearty with sour cream and chives, all set off by a green salad and a fine burgundy.

"You want dessert?" he asked, pouring the last of the wine as the fire winked and sputtered.

"Lowell, this whole evening has been dessert. I'm not used to all this, really. You're treating me like—well, I feel like I'm in a movie, and we're high up in a castle with no one else for miles around and you're the prince and—"

He leaned over and kissed her again, longer this

time. Then he finished her thought. "And I've come to wake up Sleeping Beauty and take her to my kingdom."

"Oh yes, but not Sleeping Beauty. Then we'd have to deal with all the flies, pot boys, grooms, and courtiers all waking up with me. Let's see. You've come to rescue me, and you've climbed the glass mountain and got rid of the trolls and other suitors. You're disguised as a skier, but anyone can see you're really a prince. I'm in disguise, too, and if you guess my real name, you win me and half the kingdom."

"Only half?"

"Well, you can have it all, I guess. It's only a few acres of scrub and a battered castle, and your kingdom is ten times richer to begin with."

"Oh, I don't know. It probably turns out that there's a gold mine underneath that you don't even know about, but my spies have discovered it."

"That's very underhanded," she laughed, "but all right. You've got it."

She woke the next morning feeling woozy and contented. The blankets were half on the floor, and too much light poured in from the windows. Faint humming and showering sounds issued from the bathroom. Memory flooded back unevenly, all those kisses, whispers, caresses. The yelp when she got her ankle twisted in the sheet, the delight, the drugged sleep. Her arm felt cramped, but she stretched languorously. She was still in the castle, it was no dream. Her head felt a little odd. Those martinis.

"Good morning, princess" came Lowell's voice.

"Need an aspirin? I got up and took three early this morning, but I didn't want to wake you."

He lounged, golden in the doorway, already showered and shaved. She wished fleetingly that he wasn't feeling quite so chipper. She wouldn't have minded an extra hour or two of sleepy dalliance. But a shower and strong black coffee revived her. Lowell's office called during breakfast to say there was a break in their Kuwait negotiations. He might have to fly over in the next couple of days.

"That's okay, Lowell. I only had a day left anyway. I can take the plane back tomorrow and get my act together for Pete."

"No way. You'll come with me. I'm not letting you out on your own. Besides, I'm claiming my prize. Remember? I rescued the princess so I get to marry her. Mother and Dad will have a fit, but they'll love you. Don't worry."

"Don't joke, Lowell." Damn his charm. "I've had the nicest time of my life and maybe we'll go on seeing each other, but—"

"You're afraid I'll turn into a frog!"

"Never. No, I'm afraid I will. Oh—let's be serious. We're so different, really."

She was standing at the kitchen window feeling suddenly bleak. He took her shoulders and turned her toward him, then kissed her. Still holding her, he whispered, "I'm sorry, Andrea. I didn't mean to sound flippant. Really, I've never felt this way about anyone. Sure, we're different. Isn't that part of it? We're both complicated but in different ways. I've done a few things I'm not terribly proud of, but I'd be proud to have you as my wife."

She was almost in tears. It was all happening too fast, but he looked so handsome, so vulnerable. If she hesitated, she might lose him ... but this was crazy!

"Lowell—dear Lowell. What can I say? You're the most exciting man I've ever met. But I don't know. I just can't think that quickly. Please, let's just take things a little easier for a while. Please, Lowell."

"Oh, all right. I promise. But you can't keep me from trying. Seriously, Andrea, I've never asked anyone before. I don't think I even meant to this time, but the minute I did I knew it was right. Meanwhile, let's get back to Stowe. You can watch me do a perfect run down National, and then I'll take you at backgammon." She gave him the Andy grin. It would be all right. He wasn't going to disappear. Meanwhile, she could get to know him better and see how she truly felt.

While Lowell skied, she basked in the sun. The slopes would be all slush tomorrow if a freeze hit the melt. She was reading the book Pete had given her, *Common Ground*, and became absorbed in the accounts of civil-rights clashes among blacks, Irish, and Wasps in Boston during the sixties. Then the elegant Curtis vowels cut through her concentration.

"Not a love story, I'd say by your frown. Mother says girls should avoid reading anything too serious. Bad for the complexion. Lines and all that."

"Oh, great! You're really making me anxious to

meet the gang on Beacon Hill. Don't you have any black sheep I can identify with besides Uncle Binky?"

"Well"—he paused for a moment—"there is my kid brother, Roby. It's been so long since the prodigal turned up, I guess I forgot to mention him."

"Gosh, that bad, eh? Let's see. He's a drug-addicted, left-wing ballet dancer."

Lowell was not amused. "Not far off, Andrea. He's got Mother's looks like me, only skinnier. But I used to wonder if Mums once had a secret blighted affair with an Irish bootlegger. There's something wild about him. I mean, sowing wild oats are fine when you're young, but he thinks young is forever.

"Anyway, he dropped out of college in his second year and went to New York to be an actor. He did a lot of far-out stuff in the East Village, now reviewed in the *Globe* or even the *Tribune*. Now I hear he's had some success as a singer, you know, writes his own stuff, plays the guitar. The worst was the time he arrived with his 'wife,' a little Puerto Rican girl, but Mother wouldn't let them in, so he left. I heard they'd split up, thank God."

"Why thank God? Did you meet her? She's probably a Ph.D. from Columbia. Anyway, he sounds interesting. He must be if he's anything like you."

Lowell, mollified, kissed her warmly and firmly changed the subject.

That night they had a long, luxurious dinner at Chez Bernice. Lowell had insisted. "It's our five-day anniversary." Over dinner, he presented her with a little box, beautifully wrapped. She hoped fervently that it wasn't something so personal or expensive that she would have to refuse it. With difficulty, she undid the tiny ribbons and silver paper to reveal a box containing a small paperweight with Mount Mansfield in the snow.

"Shake it, Andrea. It's supposed to remind you of me racing to your rescue."

She shook it and as she watched the lovely false flakes descending slowly, she glowed like a little girl on Christmas morning. It was exactly right. She pictured him combing the little town or even Burlington for just the perfect momento.

"Where did you find it? It's beautiful."

"Well, if you must know, Ms. Ferguson, I found it in the gas station yesterday. They had a few snowmen, too. Do I lose all my points?"

"Not one. You just know when something's right, don't you? You don't even hesitate."

He gave her his slow, blue-eyed look and said, "Exactly. And I get what I want—most of the time. . . ."

Andy slept deeply that night with her gift on the bedside table. She woke and smiled seeing it and hurried into her city clothes. Since she'd taken the train up to Vermont, she gladly accepted Lowell's offer of a ride home. He drove expertly, if a little too fast around the corners.

"Wow!" she said, expelling a nervous breath. "If I tried that in my VW, I'd be down in the gulch upside down."

"Never fear," he said, smiling. "I only take risks I can handle." When he dropped her off at Linneaen Street, she felt suddenly shy.

"Uh, Lowell, I'd ask you up but my cupboards are bare right now. Besides, we're both beat. You must be. Anyway, it was wonderful. I mean, well, thanks for everything."

Lowell let her stumble along, then reached over and gave her a firm, lingering kiss.

"If you think for a second this was only a ski romance, you're dead wrong. I'm mad about you, Andrea, and you know it. Call you when I get home. We'll decide where to meet tomorrow." He saluted and drove down the narrow street in sleek blue glory, leaving Andy smiling and still dazed.

The next evening they drove out to a place in Marblehead, where they ran into some of Lowell's sailing cronies at the bar. Andy felt caught in the middle of nautical terms totally foreign to her. Lowell beamed and plotted race tactics with obvious enthusiasm. When they ordered a second round, she declined. Then Andy decided to break the ice and turned to the pretty woman who was dressed in a leather suit with mink trim.

"Is this where you usually hang out?"

"Oh no. Denny's on the regatta committee. He, Lowell, and Dex are all members. How do you know Lowell?"

"Well, actually, I don't really. I mean, we met up at Stowe last week, well, almost a week ago."

"Lucky you. I wish I'd been up there."

What did she mean by that? Andy wondered. She's awfully cute but not long on subtlety.

Lowell turned to join them. "What's that about Stowe? Andrea, do you know Gee Gee Shurcliff?"

"Well, now I do. Nice to meet you."

Gee Gee smiled teasingly at Lowell.

"You must have had quite a time up there. I understand Jason loaned you his chalet. Isn't it just perfect?"

The last question was addressed to Andy, who was not sure what to reply. She sipped her watery drink.

"Andrea had a fall on Goat, and I just happened to be the nearest help. She was staying at the Top Notch Lodge."

"Isn't that a singles place?" asked Gee Gee.

"My boss recommended it," said Andy. "Maybe because I'm single. I'm from Denver, and I've missed skiing."

"Oh, that's nice. Did you know Kydie Allen? She married Mike Biddle, but I hear they're in splitsville. She went to a shrink, who said he was bad for her ego. She's filthy rich, of course, but Mike's almost as cute as Lowell."

She laughed and was interrupted by Denny who told Gee Gee that he was ready to leave.

"Come on, Denny. Let's stay a little longer. Have a drink. You can meet Lowell's newest flame."

Lowell quickly excused himself and Andy and located a table near the window.

"Thanks, Lowell. Another five minutes with that bimbo and I would have launched into animal rights. I'm surprised she didn't have an alligator bag and snakeskin shoes."

"Oh, Gee Gee's all right. Her husband went off with her best friend about a year ago and she's still trying to get back."

"You mean back to him or back at the whole sisterhood."

"Both. But Denny seems smitten. Not as good a catch as old Langdon, but he's easier going."

"Not as good a catch? Do people still think that way? It's Jane Austenville. She implied that you are every girl's dream—or should I say prize haddock?"

Lowell was not amused.

"I'm sorry, Lowell. I guess I just got my fur rubbed the wrong way. You are the prize. Couldn't you be a little less gorgeous?"

"Well," he smiled, "my looks are an accident, but my charm is my own creation. I've seen dozens of Gee Gees come and go for years but only one Andrea, and you've caught me. Speaking of that, why don't we order the salmon with an endive salad and a *pouilly fumeé*? Sound okay?"

"You're the food expert. If we keep seeing each other, I may have to give up hot dogs and cheese puffs. Then you better explain this regatta thing. I remember reading about it last summer."

They drove home early. Andy was due in the office at nine the next morning. Lowell insisted on walking her to her door.

"Andrea, darling, I've got to fly to Kuwait tomorrow and—"

"Why didn't you tell me?" She looked stricken.

"I didn't want to wreck the evening. What a time they pick. But it's all part of the excitement. If I can put this together, it'll be a major breakthrough for the bank. You understand, Andrea. Anyway, I'll be back Wednesday night, and Thursday we're dining at The Ritz. It's all set."

"Well, yes, that'll be lovely. Take good care of yourself, Lowell. I'll—well, I'll miss you."

This time she kissed him quickly and turned to open the door.

"Don't forget," he whispered, "I'm going to marry you."

Andy ran upstairs, flushed and giddy. Kuwait, The Ritz, marriage. Where was her father when she needed him . . . and his advice?

The next morning she stepped briskly into Pete Steiner's office at the *Tribune*.

"Morning, boss," she said, grinning.

"Well, well, well, look at you," Pete said, pushing his bulk away from the paper-strewn desk. In his youth, Pete had spent a lot of time chasing stories. Now his time was spent at an editor's desk, and he had a healthy paunch to show for it. His brown hair was thinning, and his craggy face and gruff voice sometimes put off his colleagues, but Andy knew he had a nice smile and a kind heart. He was very good at this business, and Andy had the deepest respect for his abilities. She considered Peter her best friend and emotional anchor.

"You look like a million, Andy. Maybe I should

have taken up skiing instead of bowling. Too late now. Meet anybody exciting?"

Andy reddened and shrugged.

"Aha! I knew it. I knew that lodge was the place. I checked it out. It's about time you started going out. When do I meet the guy?"

"Well, uh, Pete, he's not exactly a guy. He's something pretty special. I mean he sort of rescued me after I turned my ankle, and we just sort of got together, and he wants to marry me."

"Hold it. Hold it. No one's gonna steal my reporter right out from under me. I got all kinds of plans for you. Marry! What did you tell him?"

"Well, nothing yet. I asked him for time. But, Pete, he's the most terrific man I've ever known—you and Dad excepted of course. He's handsome and fascinating and—"

"Does he have a job?"

"That's the problem."

"I knew it. I knew it. A good-looking ski bum. I should have known it."

"No, Pete," she said with a laugh. "It's just the opposite. His father was the head of Shamut Bank, and he's in the international division. He's flying to Kuwait today."

"Oh my God, the Curtis guy, what's his name, Cabot or Lowell? Oh yeah, the tennis player, the one who has the yacht or something."

"Just a sailboat, Pete."

"Just a sailboat, huh? You must have done more than ski. No, none of my business. Well it's your life, kid. What does he think of *this*?" Pete waved his beefy hand around the office.

"He thinks I'm good. He likes the idea of my working." She wasn't entirely sure of this as they'd never really discussed it, but the last thing she needed was Pete's doubt. More than anything she wanted a shot at a major story. He'd been hinting around at something before she left.

"Can we talk about this later, Pete? I'll treat you to a beer at the Casablanca after work."

"Okay—it's a date. Now here's what I'd like you to work on today." It was penny-ante stuff, a crooked sewer inspector. Maybe Pete was waiting for some new development.

That evening she found it difficult to write in clear, concise sentences. Her mind kept straying to more personal thought—Lowell's shoulder as he bent to adjust her skis; his hair in the sunlight; the way he smelled of wool and some light spice. Finally she gave up, showered, and got into bed with an article on the new housing crisis. Something about condos swallowing all available cheap dwellings and blacks being forced into Irish neighborhoods. She'd save that for morning. What she needed was a thriller to knock her senseless. She got up, made some milky cocoa, and flopped into bed with the latest Dick Francis, bloody doings on the racetrack. Twenty minutes later, she was out.

Tuesday and Wednesday dragged by endlessly. If only her work were more engaging. She felt like a morphine addict without a fix. It began to dawn on her that her feelings for Lowell might be serious. She went so far as to buy a new dress, emerald green silk with jagged black slashes.

THE BEST MAN

Finally Thursday arrived. Pete, sensing her nervousness, sent her home early. She spent twice her usual time getting ready. Lowell arrived early, and she jumped hearing the buoyant ring of her doorbell. She allowed herself a last once-over and let him in. He stared at her for a moment, then bowed and kissed her hand.

"You look beautiful. All in silk my Andrea goes. Come on, love, I want to brag about my conquests and show you off at The Ritz bar."

She agreed to a dry martini, feeling as though she might need it. At dinner he attempted to explain the whole knotty Kuwait deal lacing it with funny anecdotes, chiefly about culture clashes. She wished she could have been there to watch him outwit the wily sheik. She could write it up. Pete would love it. Andy Ferguson, foreign correspondent. In the midst of these reveries, she saw Lowell reach into an inside pocket and produce a tiny leather box.

"It belonged to my grandmother" he said solemnly. "I chose this place because it's where it was first worn. It's not quite as big as The Ritz but close."

She stared at the huge diamond in its ornate setting.

"Oh, Lowell ... Oh, my dear Lowell, I could never. I wouldn't, I just couldn't..."

"I was afraid you'd say that," he laughed. "Okay, we'll keep it for our twentieth anniversary. Does this mean that you will marry me, Andrea darling?"

There were tears in her eyes mixed up with a lopsided grin. "You're terrible, Lowell."

He beamed. "Let's have a bottle of champagne!"

"No, no." She raised her hands in self-defense. "I've got work in the morning."

"All right, my sweet. Champagne tomorrow and we'll pick out whichever ring you choose."

In the next weeks, Andy was distracted. Pete mumbled something from time to time but didn't intrude beyond that. When their schedules allowed, Andy met Lowell at the Cambridge Tennis Club. They turned out to be well matched—he more skillful, she more daring. Now it was Saturday and a time for plans.

She unzipped her weathered duffel, pulled out a white shirt and shorts, and changed hurriedly. The green leather couches on the upper level were filled with young men and women, some in warm-up suits, others in required tennis whites. They were all deep in conversation. Lowell wasn't anywhere. She dodged the large gold trophy that dominated the room and headed for the front desk.

"Is Lowell Curtis here yet?" she asked.

"Mr. Curtis is here, Miss Ferguson. You're on court three." Andy dashed down the stairs to where Lowell was waiting.

"I'm so sorry I'm late. I got held up at the laundromat. It's rush, rush, rush all week at the *Tribune*, especially now that the Sorley-Bradford campaign is on. But that's no excuse. On weekends there's just too much to do."

Lowell looked down at Andy's feet and laughed. "Andrea Ferguson, soon to be Curtis, your socks don't match. I'm going to have to give you a head-to-toe inspection before we break the news to my family."

Sure enough, one small pom-pom was dark blue, the other dark green. She had noticed but was too rushed to care.

"Come on, Lowell. We've only signed up for an hour. We'll talk about it at lunch."

Lowell opened a new can of balls, handing one to Andy. She ran to the other side of the court. They warmed up briefly. Andy's strokes were strong and sure, but Lowell's form was superior.

"Are you ready, star reporter?" yelled Lowell, smiling.

"I sure am, banker boy" she shouted back, reaching for an overhead.

"Okay up or down?"

"Up," said Andy, "always up for me."

Lowell twirled his racquet, caught it, and checked the name on the handle end.

"It's down. Sorry, Supergirl. I win the first serve."

Lowell's serve socked in low and fast, just at the line. Andy barely returned it but managed to hit two nice cross-court shots to gain the next two points.

"You've been taking lessons from Steffi Graf," teased Lowell and proceeded to win the game.

"Darn it," muttered Andy as they changed sides. "I thought I had you."

"Oh, you have me," he whispered, "for better or

for worse. Tell you what—if you ever beat me at tennis, I'll let you out of our engagement, but that'll be when hell freezes over."

"That's not fair. You're killing my incentive. Let's say if I beat you, you promise to spend a week with me at Daddy's old ranch. I told you, it's mine now."

"What?" said Lowell, with a look of mock horror. "With no telephone, and only an outdoor privy? No way! Go ahead. Serve 'em up." They finished at 6–4, Lowell's favor.

"Hurry up, darling," he said. "We'll grab a bite at The Harvest." Andy was the first one ready, showered, dressed, with a dash of lipstick and the flick of a comb through her natural curls. She was hungry.

THREE

As they walked into the trendy restaurant off Brattle Street, Andy noticed how the women around the large, circular bar turned to stare at Lowell. Andy didn't blame them. She already knew that Lowell Curtis was, in their terminology, a catch. He was also a member of a world she had never known and was a bit intimidated by. She wasn't used to the restaurant scene. When she was at college in New York, Andy always ate in small coffee houses with her fellow graduate students. The atmosphere was casual, and they could comfortably gorge on potato skins at the cocktail hour and call it dinner.

What did Lowell see in her? An unsophisticated reporter whose happiest times had been spent with her father on a tumbledown ranch in Colorado? Lowell said she underestimated her own freshness, a subtle beauty, and an inner strength that the lounge lizards lacked.

A redhead at the bar waved furiously. Lowell smiled. He took Andy by the hand and led the way to the woman. "Andrea, this is Tami Hartwick. Tami, I'd like you to meet Andrea Ferguson."

Andy shook hands, but Tami ignored her and looked straight at Lowell. "Hi, handsome. We haven't seen you around lately. Skip says the Beachcomber isn't the same without you."

"I've been preoccupied, Tami," said Lowell, squeezing Andy's hand. Andy felt like a sack of potatoes, standing beside Lowell. She shifted from one foot to the other, but Lowell didn't seem to mind.

"See you on the circuit, Tami," he said as he turned to Andy. Lowell looked so handsome in his blue blazer, with his blond hair slicked back. His tall, manicured good looks seemed in direct contrast to Andy's rosy cheeks, damp curls, and casual blouse and sweater. Andy decided not to ask about Tami.

"Let's eat in Bill's Café," said Lowell. "I like those wild Marimekko fabrics on the walls. Besides, it's much friendlier than that big formal dining room."

Andy looked up at Lowell. It was the first time in two years that anyone had taken care of her. She had been the man in the family after her father died, watching over her mother and little sister. But now this knight was giving the orders. It was different, very different, but she found it strangely comforting.

"I've never been here before. My gang always eats at The Acropolis. Who's Bill, anyway?"

Lowell laughed. "Always the reporter, aren't you? Bill is Bill Thompson. He's the architect who designed Quincy Marketplace. He built this, too."

"Good afternoon, Mr. Curtis," said an approaching waiter. "Will there be two today?"

"Good heavens, Lowell!" Andy exclaimed. "Does everybody know you?"

"Making oneself known is part of being an international banker, I guess," said Lowell. "But here's a little confession. There was a mad Israeli pianist who used to love this place. I always brought him here after the concerts, and I guess we became pretty well known." Lowell turned to the waiter. "Two in the far corner, if possible."

"Just follow me, Mr. Curtis."

Lowell stood up until Andy was seated.

"Lowell, you spoil me with your good manners. I'm used to the *Tribune*, where I'm treated like one of the guys."

"I guess the family has always put a heavy accent on manners," said Lowell. "I remember the year when I was at Le Rosey, I spent Christmas in Paris with Grandmother. She had a small apartment in the sixteenth arrondissement and a good friend, François, who used to take her to theater, opera, all that stuff. When I came, the three of us used to go out to dinner.

"I remember once Grandmother announced we would have dinner at La Grande Finale, a one-star restaurant on Ile de la Cité. We walked in, or rather, François and I walked in; Grandmother *swept* in. She was tall, like Mummy, and majestic. I followed the waiter to the table and sat down immediately. François held Grandmother's chair. 'No, darling,' Grandmother said to François. 'If Lowell wants to come with us to dinner he must learn some proper manners. A gentleman always holds the chair for the lady and never sits down until she does. Now get up, Lowell, and come here.' I never forgot that, but then, Grandmother had a persuasive way about her. Grandmother ruled the roost. That was the year I learned about wines, too. Grandmother had salons every Thursday afternoon from four to six. I went to them when I was on vacation. She'd have a smattering of ambassadors, some musicians, and writers. She'd serve ghastly little sandwiches, warm orange squash, and wonderful white wines. That was it. But I learned about wines."

Andy looked at Lowell. He was thoroughly enjoying himself, discoursing about his time in France, his grandmother, and her lover— Andy guessed François was her lover. Lowell's life had been so different from hers. She'd been to Colorado, New York, and Boston, but never to Europe. Nobody in her family had: not Ben Ferguson, buried in his Timberline Press; not her mother, though she'd complained about it enough; and not Amy, who'd wanted to study there but was unable to because of the cost.

As for grandmothers with lovers—no Ferguson had ever been that daring, and if a Littleton had strayed, nobody ever talked about it. Lowell seemed to relish all of this—lovers, France, wines.

He was so sophisticated. Could Andy ever be part of Lowell's world? Obviously, he thought so. Andy, direct as always, decided to plunge in.

"Lowell, that woman you introduced me to was talking about The Beachcomber. What is it?"

"Oh, that's the bar I told you about that Skip's running. He tried a position at Sullivan and Pierce for two years after law school, but he hated it. So a bunch of us got together and backed him in this bar. He's made a big success of it. All our pals go there. There's a rinky-dink piano and sometimes we just hang out and sing Hasty Pudding songs. I'll take you there sometime. You'll love it."

"I'm not big on bars, but I'd be willing to give The Beachcomber a try. I'll tell the guys at the *Trib* about it." Andy felt more on home territory talking about her paper, her colleagues, and her job. "You should have heard the commotion yesterday. The paper's backing Tom Bradford against that awful Gene Sorley. It's going to be a hot race, but Pete Steiner thinks he has a chance."

"Tom Bradford. Really! I don't like the cut of his jib. Anyway, Andrea, now that we've, a-hem, declared our intentions, you're going to have a lot to think about besides your career."

"Marrying you, it's still kind of overwhelming, but this much I know. I've been trained in journalism and I'm good at it. I love my job, and I intend to stay with it as long as they'll have me."

Lowell smiled. "I admire your spunk, Andrea. Now let's talk about something important, like what we're going to have for lunch." Lowell looked at the bright yellow menu. "Darling, would you like baked scrod or grilled halibut?"

"Why don't you order for me, Lowell. I—we've got so much to talk about, I just can't concentrate on food. I'd just as soon have a grilled cheese."

"Live and learn, my Rocky Mountain beauty. We'll have two halibut, grilled, and a bottle of Vouvray fifty-five," said Lowell to the waiter. Then he turned to Andy. "Okay darling. No more grilled cheese for you. And the Vouvray is pleasant and gentle. It really tastes more like an excellent cider than a wine. Now, I'm all yours."

"Not quite yet, Mr. Curtis. Before we do anything else, before I learn all about Vouvrays and The Beachcomber, we've just got to tell our parents what's happened. Mom's been asking questions ever since I told her I met an attractive man in a snow drift in Stowe."

"You're right, sweetheart. Mother and Daddy haven't said boo, but their nosy Maureen cleans my Marlborough Street pad, and I'm certain she's reported the recent influx of Dewar's and forgotten tennis rackets and reporter's notebooks to those Beacon Hill inhabitants."

Andy, who furnished her rented apartment with secondhand couches and chairs, who had never had the time or inclination to decorate, continued to marvel at Lowell's so-called pad. It was crammed with memorabilia, family portraits, family silver, a needlepoint pillow his mother had lovingly stitched for him, and a footstool of his grandmother's.

Lowell noticed Andy was frowning. "What's the matter, darling?"

"Do you think your parents will be hurt because I don't want your grandmother's engagement ring?"

"Probably, but after we've had our two summit meetings, at least you'll be able to wear the one we picked out."

Andy reached in her blouse and pulled out a thin gold chain with the ring she had chosen on it. She unhooked the chain and took off the ring. Three small diamond chips on a plain gold band. She gave it to Lowell.

"We've had secrets long enough," she grinned—that famous Ferguson grin that lit up the room.

Lowell reached across the table and put the ring on the third finger of her left hand.

"Finally," he said. "Now when do we break the news?"

"I'm having Sunday brunch with Mom and Amy tomorrow. I haven't seen them in weeks. I'll tell them then. I know Mom will be thrilled. Amy will probably be green with envy."

"You handle that, Andrea. Just like you handle everything. I'll tell the family to hold Wednesday. How about that?"

"Wednesday's my toughest day at the *Tribune*. That's when we wind up the Weekend Section. Can't you make it Thursday?"

"Someday, my dear, I'll teach you to keep bankers' hours. But this time you get your way. I'll tell Mother and Daddy I'm bringing a young lady to dinner on Thursday night."

* * *

Andy ran up the flagstone walk of her mother's white brick, one-storied house in an exclusive section of Newton. The yard was neat and well-kept, and the picture window was framed with low evergreens.

The whole place reeked of new money and conventionality to Andy. This never would be home to her. Home to her was still back in the snow-capped mountains and aspen groves, but with Lowell she was finally putting all that behind her. At least Uncle Simon Littleton had the good sense to die and leave a large enough bequest so her mother could move back East, "where she belonged." Andy was ambivalent. She was happy that Grace had finally achieved the status she wanted for herself and Amy, but they hardly ever talked about the old life . . . or Ben. And that made her sad.

She rang the bell. A perky blonde with a cheerleader figure opened the door. She was wearing a mauve cowl-necked cashmere sweater and purple suede pants.

"Hi, stranger," said Amy. "I haven't seen you in ages. We've hardly had a word since you got that 'Painting the Town' column."

Andy, as always, felt oafish beside her younger sister. Even after having Lowell in her life, she envied Amy's ease with the social graces.

"Well, I've been pretty busy with my column—and other things."

"What other things? Come on, Andrea. You've never been a woman of mystery." Amy, like her mother and Lowell, insisted on calling her Andrea. "I remember when you applied for that scholarship to Columbia's School of Journalism. You stewed for months over that series on strip mining in the Rockies. You and Dad would talk about it every night at dinner and bore the daylights out of me and Mom."

Amy followed Andy into the living room. A pale wall-to-wall carpet covered the floor. Pillows of the same shade accented the peach-and-blue chintzes on the couch and wing chair. The space had a new, decorated look. A dining room filled with Grand Rapids reproductions was off to the left, and a pristine eat-in kitchen lay beyond. The fake Chippendale dining room table was set for three.

"Why are we eating in the dining room instead of the kitchen?"

"Well, Andrea. You've been so evasive that Mom smelled a rat. I told her I was sure you wouldn't have insisted on this brunch unless you had been transferred to the Paris office."

"Paris isn't in the picture for me right now, Amy. But tell me, how's your interior decorating course coming? You're the one who could go whipping to Paris to pick out fabrics if you landed with some big-deal firm."

"Sometimes I think it's too much like work, Andrea. That TV modeling would have suited me fine. If only I hadn't been too short."

"Amy, you could have a high-powered career as a decorator."

"You're the career woman. It's hard to concentrate on all those dumb books after I've been partying."

A high, strident voice broke up the dialogue between the two sisters.

"Amy, was that Andrea at the door?"

"Yes, Mom—and only twenty minutes late. That's pretty good for her." Grace Ferguson hurried through the dining room and gave Andy a hug and a peck on the cheek. She was short, like her younger daughter, her hair kept blond by weekly trips to the beauty parlor. She wore a black wool sheath, which she and Amy had picked out together, and a heavy gold necklace.

"Andrea, darling. What a special treat. I've been looking forward to this all week. I even made Amy stay home from a reunion with some Conn College friends so we could all have this time together."

"Thanks to both of you for being here. Let's go into the kitchen and sit around the table. I have some really big news." Andy, looking taller and slimmer than ever in her formal pumps, led the way. In the center of the kitchen's terra cotta–tiled floor was a large oval island with stools around it. As they sat down, Amy poked Andy in the back. Even at twenty-two, she was still playing the part of little sister. "Tell me what's going on," she commanded.

"Come on, dear," prompted her mother. "Is it a big promotion or—or could it be something else? Don't keep us in suspense."

"Okay. I know you two have been suspecting plenty. But it's not about my job at all. That's going fine. Not that this isn't fine. It's just that everything happened so fast. I—I just wanted to be sure before I told you. But then, does anybody know for certain? Did you know right away when Dad interviewed you for the *Denver Courier* when you were singing in Boulder? Did you know that he was the one for you?"

"Of course not, dear. I thought he was very attractive, but it took time. We waited until I graduated, you know. Oh, Andrea," she added, "I hope you're not involved with an idealistic, penniless journalist."

"Whoopee, Andrea's got a guy," shouted Amy. She pulled up a stool and sat drumming her fingers on the butcher block. "Who is he? Tell, tell, tell."

Andy realized she was about to drop a bombshell. The idea of Lowell would send Grace spinning. She would think that Andy had at last turned her back on Colorado and the Blue Ridge Ranch. What Grace would never understand was that it was Lowell's magnetic charm, his wit, the electricity she felt when he held her, the new world that he brought to her—these were the things that mattered. His social position and money didn't impress her one bit. Amy, of course, would flip. For all the wrong reasons.

"Well," said Andy slowly, "do you remember that week in February when I took off and went to Stowe to get away from it all?"

"Sure," said Amy. "That's when you sprained your ankle."

"Well, to tell you the truth, that was only the half of it. Early Monday morning I rented some skis and after a few runs down the intermediate slopes I decided to go for the Goat."

"You're crazy," said Amy. "Why, that's one of the biggies."

"Can't compare to Ajax in Aspen. Dad and I used to go down that all the time."

"Yes, I remember, dear," said Grace, hardly able to contain herself. "What happened?"

"Well, I was about halfway down, when I hit a mogul and—*foom*—my skis went out from under me. I lay spread-eagled in the snow. When I tried to get up my ankle felt like someone was throwing knives in it. I just sat in the snow, not knowing what to do next when up skied this tall, blond, gorgeous guy."

"How old?" asked Amy.

"Thirty, Miss Nosy. He stopped and asked if I was okay. When I said my ankle hurt, he said not to worry. He'd get the ski patrol and meet me at the bottom of the slope. And away he whizzed. I didn't know whether or not I'd ever see him again."

"Yes, dear," said Grace, "Go on."

"The ski patrol came in about fifteen minutes. They brought me to the bottom of the mountain on a stretcher, and there he was. My angel of mercy."

"Who?" said mother and daughter, practically in unison.

"Lowell Curtis."

"Lowell Curtis, Henry Curtis's son?"

"That's the one, Mom. Mr. Curtis is retired now

and Lowell is with the international division of the First Shamut Bank."

"I saw his picture in the *Boston Globe* accepting the Faulk Tennis Trophy at Longwood," said Amy.

"We carried that picture, too," said Andy, feeling a sibling antagonism from long ago she could not explain.

"Girls, girls," said Grace as she pulled a stool up beside Andy. "Please let Andrea finish."

"Well, he told me I was the most delightful, bedraggled snow maiden he's ever met."

"That's a compliment?" asked Amy.

Andy blushed. Grace, sensing the static between her two daughters, jumped up and quickly started pouring mugs of coffee.

"Thanks for the coffee," Andy said. She could tell that her mother was proud.

"Of course it was meant as a compliment," said Grace with a chiding glance at Amy. Andy plunged on. "Well, that very night he asked me to have dinner with him at Chez Bernice. Me, Andy Ferguson, with my scraped chin and strapped ankle."

"I've heard of that place," chimed Amy. "It's about twenty miles from Stowe. A friend from Conn went there with a guy from Trinity. She said it was really romantic."

Andy wondered who else Lowell had taken there, but that didn't matter now.

Grace glared. Just as excited as her younger daughter, she had learned more restraint. "Amy, stop interrupting. Please let Andrea talk."

"Well, we had dinner that night. He really knows wines. He ordered a Château Gris. I'd never heard of it. It's from the region of St. George's. Lowell lived there for a time." Andy knew Grace would approve of that.

"Then I'll bet he's a good sailor," said Amy. "I used to go to Newport with my friends sometimes on weekends, and I'd see all those kids out there practicing. Does he have a yacht?"

"Amy, he's only thirty," said Grace.

"We talked about lots of things at dinner. He told me he'd been in the chorus line of the Hasty Pudding show at Harvard, and that he loves show tunes, especially Cole Porter."

"Cole Porter," sighed Grace. "How sweet and old-fashioned."

"He just likes to sing, Mom. I've heard him. He has a really good tenor voice. He told me he reads my column sometimes. That was important to me. He said he liked my style. The evening just flew by. He even gave me a tape of 'Ella Sings Cole' with a card that said 'You're the Top.' "

"Oh, Andrea," said Amy, "That's *so-o* romantic."

"I thought so, too, Amy," said Andy, happy to agree with her about something. "Well, we spent almost the whole week together. He even taught me to play backgammon. One game I threw three doubles in a row and beat him. 'Maybe you'll get really lucky and marry me,' he said. And then, two days later, he proposed."

"And then?" said Grace, her eyes sparkling.

"Well," said Andy, deciding to delete the night at Jason's chalet, "I—I was bowled over. Andrea Ferguson, former scholarship student at Columbia's School of Journalism married to Lowell Curtis, international wheeler and dealer. I told him I needed some time to think it over."

What Andy didn't tell them was how much she had needed her father to talk to. He'd see right through all the superficial touches that meant so much to Grace and Amy. He'd see right to the core of Lowell. She desperately hoped he'd agree with her decision. There's no doubt he would have told her if he hadn't.

"Andrea," said Amy. "I just can't believe you. Here you are, about to land the catch of Boston, and you need time to think it over. What's to think over? You'll never have to work another day in your life. You can go skiing at the Klosters, sailing in the Caribbean . . ."

Andy looked directly at Amy. "Please understand. I want you both to see where I'm coming from. I'm just starting the assignments I've always dreamed of. I love writing. I love newspapers. It's been the most meaningful part of my life up until now. Pete Steiner says I have a real talent. Who knows? I might even win a Pulitzer someday. I told Lowell I didn't want my marriage to jeopardize my career."

"You didn't," said Grace in an amazed tone.

"Lowell understood, or he said he did. He said he'd wait. We've been together almost every night these past two months. It's been magical. I didn't want to let on to Pete and the guys, but I know I've been daydreaming too much. We've been to the symphony, and you both know that's not my bag. Lowell even took me to an after-symphony party at the Haits to meet the artist. Lowell knows all the performers. That awful Gene Sorley was there. I almost died."

"Music is a part of the Curtises' life, dear," said Grace. "His family has had a box for generations. I remember Uncle Simon telling me that Mrs. Curtis was always there with her golden-haired little boy."

Andy laughed. "Yep, that was Lowell. He told me his mother always made him sit in front of her, and she'd pinch him if he started to go to sleep. He likes tennis, too, and that's much more up my alley. He plays a wicked game."

"Well, you're no slouch," said Amy.

"No. Just rusty. We've been playing almost every day after work. He always beats me. Then he jumps over the net and says, 'Are you ready to marry me?' I don't know if I'm ready to marry anybody, but he just swept me off my feet. Last Saturday I gave in."

"You mean you hooked Lowell Curtis last Saturday and you haven't told us for a whole week?" said Amy in amazement.

"He's not a fish, Amy. It all just sort of happened, boom. I still can't believe it."

Andy looked at her pert sister, her elegant clothes covering her rounded body, so different from her own slim frame. She remembered so many telephone conversations between Amy and her sorority friends. "Are you pinned yet?" "I know I'm going to be homecoming queen." "If you wear that black-and-white-striped dress, you'll nab him for keeps." Popular Amy and all her games—she would never change.

"Amy, dear, let Andrea finish," said Grace.

"There really isn't that much more to say, Mom. We were on court three. That's the court Lowell always tries to get because the lighting's better. I kept serving double faults. I just couldn't seem to hit the dumb ball over the net. Lowell asked me what was the matter. I—I just blurted out I'd marry him. He picked me up and whirled me around the court and the deed was done!"

Andy reached in her purse, unzipped the back pocket, and took out her engagement ring. She put it on and waved her hand in the air.

"Andrea, you and Lowell Curtis. I just can't believe it," screamed Amy. "Let me see the ring."

Andy walked over and held out her hand to Amy.

"Oh, it's beautiful. But if it had been me, I would have asked for a much bigger diamond."

"Those things never interested Andrea, Amy. You know that," said Grace. "Your time will come." She rushed over to Andy and gave her a big hug. "Oh, Andrea dear, this is all wonderful. I have one bottle of Korbel left over from New Year's. Let's open it right now. Amy, go get the champagne glasses out of the dining room cabinet."

"Sure, I'll open the champagne, Mom," said Amy. "Andrea, you just sit down and do nothing. Make like a bride."

Make like a bride. To Amy that meant clothes and decorating and more parties. In her heart of hearts Andy knew that Amy would never take a career seriously, but she kept on hoping. She'd try to explain her thinking once more.

"Amy, I just can't sit around and do nothing. I'm going to stay at the *Trib*, Lowell knows that. I plan to work up to senior reporter."

"You do?"

"Well, that's just fine," said Grace, sounding as though it would be better not to tackle Andy on this point just yet. "But, dear, I hope that now that you're going to be a Curtis, you'll give up that boyish nickname."

"No way. I like it and Pete thinks it throws the readers off balance."

"You sound just like your father," said Grace. "Come on, Amy. Bring the bottle right over here. I want to hear the pop when you open it."

"Thar she blows."

"Good, Amy. Now fill up our glasses."

Grace stood up, faced her taller daughter, and raised her glass. "Here's to you, Andrea. Here's to you and Lowell, I should say."

Andy took a sip and then turned to her mother and sister. "And here's one for Daddy. I hope he would approve."

Grace couldn't hide her jubilance. "Oh, honey. I knew I was right to come back East. I never wanted you and Amy to get stuck in a Denver suburb like I did. Buying this house with Uncle Simon's money was the smartest move I've ever made. A Curtis. Goodness, Andrea. They must be worth I don't know what."

Listening to her mother, Andy understood only too well why Ben had spent so much time at the ranch. She had her disappointments, but Ben certainly had his.

Andy paced across the kitchen and wheeled around. "Mother, Lowell and I love each other. That's what's important."

"Of course it is, dear. But we must do things properly. That's what the Curtises will expect. We'll have the engagement party here. You'll be married at Trinity Church, of course, in June."

"And I'll be the maid of honor," piped up Amy.

"Of course you will, Amy, but, hey, let's go slow. I haven't given any of this a thought."

Grace continued, living out her own fantasies of the wedding she'd never been able to have. "And the reception will be at The Ritz."

Andy was horrified. "The Ritz? Mom, you can't swing that. Anyway, Lowell and I haven't discussed any of this. We haven't even told his parents."

Grace patted Andy's hand. "It isn't every day my daughter marries a Curtis. The Littletons left me in good shape. The Ritz it will be, but no more than two hundred fifty guests."

Andy took a deep breath. A fine time to have given up smoking. She yearned for a drag. "Please, Mom. Cool it. I don't know half that many people. I just want my *Trib* co-workers and a few buddies from journalism school. I hope Richard Kotuk will come. He's the best teacher I ever had. . . . "

"You have to think about Lowell, Andrea," said Amy, who had kept silent for an unusually long time. "He'll want to have all his prep school and college friends plus all the Curtis family. You'll be *lucky* to keep it to two hundred and fifty."

"I'll tell you what, dear," said Grace, trying to avoid a stalemate. We'll wait until we meet with the Curtises to discuss a guest list. But I'll order a batch of invitations. They take at least three weeks to be engraved."

"Engraved! That's ridiculous, Mom. I can get them done in offset much cheaper through the paper."

"No daughter of mine will have anything but engraved invitations."

The whole thing was getting out of hand. She put her hands over her face. "This is supposed to be such a happy time and all we're doing is fighting," she wailed.

"Andrea's right, Mom," said Amy. Amy, who never disagreed with her mother about social arrangements, hated to see Andy, her protector, so upset.

"If I were marrying Lowell Curtis I'd be dancing on the ceiling. Tell you what. You and Andrea go in the living room and talk. I'll wrestle with the brunch."

Andy looked at Amy gratefully. "Thanks for getting us back on the track, kid. Come on, Mom, follow me. We'll go in the other room and have a real heart-to-heart."

Andy put her arm around her mother's waist, and together they walked into the living room. The old, familiar couches and chairs from Denver had been reupholstered by an expensive Brookline decorator. To Andy, it was a cold and overmanicured room. They sat on the couch under the portrait her mother had commissioned for her twentieth wedding anniversary. Andy was fourteen then, Amy ten. Andy, tall for her age, was dressed in a red jumper that was much too short for her. She looked ill at ease. Amy, standing beside her, was all dimples and smiles, her golden curls tumbling over a pink dress with a lace collar.

"Now, Mom," said Andy in a pacifying tone, "this is a crazy time for me. So much is going on at the *Trib* and now I've got a June wedding to plan. I really never thought it'd be this big a deal. I guess everything's happened so quickly I just haven't had time to think."

Grace took Andy's hand. She still couldn't believe that it was Andy who had fulfilled all her social ambitions, that finally she, Grace Littleton Ferguson, would be included in Boston society. She spoke slowly but purposefully. "Andrea, you've always been the independent one. Just like your father. But this is family time. The most important event in your whole life. We must all work together. We only have two months to arrange everything. The engagement party first, of course. I guess we should have music. Then the wedding itself. The flowers, the guest list, the reception. I'd better make an appointment at Priscilla's so we can pick out a wedding dress."

"I am just too busy to be in on every single detail, Mom. But you must consult me—and Lowell—before every decision."

"Listen, my headstrong child. I haven't even met

my future son-in-law, though, as you know, I heartily approve."

"I sure know that," said Andy, feeling that she was losing control. "I just feel I'm caught in a whirlwind. Lowell's introducing me to his mother and father next Thursday. He has a younger brother, too, but he never talks much about him. After I meet all the Curtises, we'll have a joint family meeting."

"That's fine with me, but right now we have to write the engagement announcement. That has to go in six weeks before the wedding."

"Not in the *Trib*. And that's all I care about. Pete will put it in the day before if somebody wants to."

"I'm not talking about the *Tribune*, Andrea. I'm talking about the *Globe* and *The New York Times*."

"Mother. I don't care about those papers. Not one bit."

"If you're marrying a Curtis, Andrea, this is what is expected."

Nothing had changed. Her mother always did just what was expected. Andy was not going to change her. She decided to appease her and go along. This would all be finished soon enough.

"Okay, Mom. I'll write it for you. Just give me a day to check with Lowell."

Andy started to write while Grace sat smugly on the couch, reading over her daughter's shoulder:

Mrs. Benjamin Ferguson of Newton Center, Massachusetts, has announced the engage-

ment of her daughter, Andrea Littleton Ferguson, to Lowell Gardner Curtis, son of Mr. and Mrs. Henry Curtis of Boston, Massachusetts. A June wedding is planned. Miss Ferguson is also the daughter of the late Benjamin Ferguson of Denver, Colorado, publisher of Timberline Press, Inc. She is a graduate of the Columbia School of Journalism and a reporter on the staff of the Boston Tribune.

Mr. Curtis, a graduate of St. George's School and Harvard College, is in the international division of the First Shamut Bank of Boston. His father, Henry Curtis, now retired, was chairman of the board.

Andy ripped the piece of paper out of her notebook and handed it to her mother. Grace read it over carefully. "Lowell Gardner Curtis and Andrea Littleton Ferguson," she murmured. "I still can't believe it. Dependable, career-minded Andrea—who would have thought?" Her mother smiled. "Yes, Andrea. That says it all."

FOUR

Andy felt thwarted her next three days at the *Trib*. While other reporters were assigned copy on the upcoming Bradford-Sorley campaign, Andy was told to cover the Swampscott Flower Show and interview a twelve-year-old boy who was saved from drowning in the Charles River by his German shepherd. As always, she did her pieces thoroughly and with verve, but Thursday, the day of the Beacon Hill dinner, came only too quickly.

On Thursday morning, Andy made an appointment to see Pete at two. Despite her frustrations, she cheered up the minute she walked into his cluttered office. Pink slips saying, PLEASE CALL were tossed helter skelter all over his desk. A white plastic container held the remnants of a hamburger and fries, and Pete was sipping a Coke through a straw.

"Afternoon, Andy. That was a good piece you did on that kid and the dog."

"Thanks, Pete."

"What can I do for you? You're not just stopping by to chew the fat. Not when you make a formal appointment."

"Actually, Pete, I was hoping you'd give me some harder news for a change," said Andy, who was aching to leap into the Bradford-Sorley fray. "But that's not why I'm here. I need a favor."

"What's that?"

"Could I get off an hour earlier? I have a big night ahead of me," said Andy, direct as always.

Pete put down his Coke and opened the top drawer of his desk. He pulled out a large, fat cigar and lit it. Andy watched as he blew a smoke ring. "Should I ask any questions?"

"Not yet, if you don't mind."

"Okay, but I'm a bloodhound at heart." Pete's phone started to ring.

"Thanks, Pete," said Andy. "See you tomorrow." She waved at Pete and was gone.

It was five o'clock when Andy arrived at her third-floor walk-up on Linneaen Street. It was a sparsely furnished apartment with beige walls, a couch, and a large, overstuffed chair of brown tweed. A small kitchen with an apartment stove and refrigerator were at one end of the living room and a cheap wooden dinette set, practically unused, was beside it. Beyond the couch was Andy's bedroom, which consisted simply of a double bed and dresser and that was all. The only decorations were framed photos of the Blue Ridge Ranch and of her and Ben.

When Andy had brought Amy and Grace to see the apartment, she could tell they were appalled by its starkness. "This looks like 'Early Motel,' Andrea," stated Amy. "Don't you care anything about appearances?"

The truth of the matter was, of course, that she didn't. She had helped her mother and sister settle into their house in Newton. She had arranged the mortgage with her bank and attended to the house insurance. After all that, she set out to find herself a place that would require absolutely no effort. She didn't have time for possessions, for little dinner parties—for a home. Her career was on its way. The apartment was only a place to sleep.

Andy threw her clothes on the unmade bed and showered quickly. The water was warm and seemed to soothe her unexpressed anxieties, but she had to hurry. There just never seemed to be enough time. She chose her dress carefully, a dark green paisley shirtwaist with a full, swirling skirt. Her natural beauty was reflected in the simple, classic dress. She wanted to please Lowell. She wanted to be at ease with the family that was so important to him. She wanted to feel secure in her decision. Andy had never been on Beacon Hill, although she had written a story about the annual tradition of Christmas caroling with eggnog served afterward. She had titled her piece "Noblesse Oblige." She was glad now that the assistant

THE BEST MAN 65

managing editor had changed it to an innocuous "Merry Christmas from Beacon Hill."

She was just switching a lipstick to her small, red, shoulder-strap purse when she heard the now-familiar knock of Lowell's.

"Come, on, sweetheart. This is it," shouted Lowell.

Andy opened the door and there he was, her husband-to-be, impeccable in a blue pinstripe suit, his lean, aristocratic face beaming a smile. She wished they could just kick off their shoes and order in Chinese.

"Lowell," she gasped. "You look wonderful."

Lowell eyed her up and down. Andy whirled around, half-teasing, half-serious. "I hope you approve," she said. What she meant was she hoped they approved.

"I love the looks of you," sang Lowell, "the lure of you..." He took her hands. "Cole must have had you in mind when he wrote that, Andrea. Now let's go. The family expects us to be on time."

Lowell ushered Andy up three steps to the brick townhouse at 25 Chestnut Street. He grabbed the handle of the lion's-head knocker that decorated the green wooden door. Andy knew how important it was to Lowell that his family approve of his choice. She wished desperately that she'd listened more to Grace's early lectures on social niceties.

"Come on, darling. Smile. I know you'll make a big hit," said Lowell. Andy wondered if he really was so sure she would. The door opened and Andy was surprised. Instead of Mrs. Curtis, a maid in a black uniform with a white apron received them.

"Good evening, Mr. Curtis," she said.

"Good evening, Maureen. This is Miss Ferguson."

"How d'ya do, ma'am? May I take your coat?"

Andy handed Maureen her London Fog and looked around. To the right of the black-and-white marble reception hall was a small parlor. It was filled with Directoire furniture. A love seat covered in pale yellow damask, a delicate armchair, and a large stool. Behind the love seat was a column with a bronze bust of Julius Caesar. An Aubusson rug graced the floor, with a pattern of yellow flowers on a rose background.

"Grandmother had all that stuff shipped here from her apartment in Paris," whispered Lowell, "after Mother decided that she was too old to be over there cavorting. Come on, let's go up."

Andy slowly ascended the spiral staircase to the second floor. To the left was a paneled library facing Chestnut Street. Books lined the walls from ceiling to floor. Andy liked the idea of the books, but they all had leather bindings. Andy wondered when they had last been read. Over a carved mantel was a portrait of a fat man with ruddy cheeks. He was bulging out of a frock coat. There was no one in the room.

"We always have Christmas in this room," said Lowell. "Only candles on the tree, no electric lights. Kind of a Curtis tradition, I guess. I hope we keep it up."

Andy, who was trying so hard to put her past

behind her, was not certain she wanted to take on somebody else's old traditions, but she said nothing.

"This way," said Lowell. He took Andy by the arm and ushered her formally into the room on the right. The evening shadows were trickling in, and Andy took in the faded green velvet couch, framed by long French windows. A heavy Lalique chandelier lit the room, and Andy noticed a black grand piano glistening in the corner. On the couch sat a large woman in a gray silk dress. She wore practically no makeup, just a hint of pink lipstick. Her face was weather-beaten, her nose thin and birdlike. Her hair was short and white. Andy guessed she was about the same age as Grace, though she looked much older. She smiled, and Andy could see a distinct resemblance to Lowell. Her gray-blue eyes did not light up, however. They looked cold and distant. Lowell stood stiffly beside Andy, his legs apart, his hands behind his back. Andy felt the tension in the air. She knew Lowell desperately wanted his mother's approval, and he was clearly uncomfortable with the situation.

"Mother, I'd like you to meet Andrea Ferguson."

Andy walked over and shook hands. Mrs. Curtis had a firm handshake.

"How do you do, Mrs. Curtis? I'm so glad to meet you. Lowell has told me such wonderful things about you."

Margaret Curtis looked at Lowell. When she did so, her whole face lit up. Her eyes, so remote when she looked at Andy, now shone. There was a special rapport between mother and son. As long as Lowell's woman didn't interfere in their special bond, Andy guessed everything would be fine with Mrs. Curtis.

"Well, Lowell and I go back a long way," said Mrs. Curtis.

Lowell, who had not moved from his Prince Philip stance, chortled at his mother's little joke.

"Lowell has told me all about your taking him to the symphony and how you would come to St. George's on Sundays and spring him for dinner at Charlie's on the wharf."

"That's nice," said Mrs. Curtis. Andy realized the evening wasn't going to be easy.

"Oh, Andrea," said Mrs. Curtis, almost as an afterthought, "this is my husband, Henry." Henry Curtis, a stocky man two inches shorter than his wife, was standing beside the couch. He had a ring of white hair around the back of his head. He looked jolly, but it seemed to Andy that Mrs. Curtis regarded him almost as an extra appendage.

"Hello, Andrea," he said. "Ever since Lowell told Mrs. Curtis and me the news, we've been talking of nothing else. I'm delighted to meet you."

Andy was amazed at the formality between husband and wife. She wondered if he always referred to her as Mrs. Curtis, not Margaret or Peggy. Lowell seemed much more free, his values more contemporary ... though his apartment on Marlborough Street was very similar to this Beacon Hill house.

"Please come sit down," said Mrs. Curtis. "Right here by me on the couch so we can have a little

THE BEST MAN 69

chat. I really want to get to know you since you're going to be one of us."

Andy walked around the red oriental coffee table and sat beside Mrs. Curtis. Henry perched himself in the cane-backed chair. Lowell finally broke his stance and sat in the wing chair. He looked at Andy and winked as if to say, "You're doing fine." But he said nothing.

"Lowell tells me some of your family's from Boston," said Mrs. Curtis. "Are you one of the Beverly Farms Fergusons? I worked with a Pamela Ferguson in the Trinity Church Altar Guild."

"No, Ferguson was my father's family. They were all from Colorado. My mother was brought up in Newton." Andy knew Margaret Curtis would have liked to hear about the grander Littleton connection, but a stubborn streak of pride stopped her from mentioning it.

"Mother, I told you Andrea's father was head of the Timberline Press. That's how Andrea got interested in journalism," said Lowell.

His long, elegant frame stretched out casually in the wing chair so he gave the appearance of being totally relaxed. But Andy noticed that his jaw was set, his temples throbbing with tension. Miraculously, Maureen appeared with a silver tray laden with decanters and glasses. She put the tray down in front of Mrs. Curtis.

"I'll do the honors, Mother," said Lowell.

"Thanks, dear," beamed Mrs. Curtis. "We'll serve our honored guest first. What would you like, Andrea?"

Andy was dying for a slug of Scotch but thought

better of it. "I'll have a sherry, Mrs. Curtis," she said.

"Me, too, Lowell," said Mrs. Curtis. "And I bet I know what you and Father will have.

"Lowell and Mr. Curtis always have martinis, straight up," said Mrs. Curtis. "You know, my family used to say there are shakers and there are stirrers. The Curtises are stirrers." Lowell poured the gin and vermouth into a pitcher on the silver tray. He dumped in ten ice cubes from the silver ice bucket and began to stir. Andy realized what a "stirrer" was and noticed that Mrs. Curtis, satisfied with her in-family reference, was watching her beloved son, oblivious of her future daughter-in-law. Lowell poured the chilled martinis into two stemmed glasses.

"Lowell, I'll have just a tad more sherry, thank you," said Mrs. Curtis. "And now, Andrea, do tell me about your job. Everything has changed so much. In my day you just made your debut and then got married. Of course, I did go to Pine Manor for two years, but I guess Lowell told you all that."

Andy realized that Lowell had not filled her in on any details of what he referred to as "the family." Her instinct told her Mrs. Curtis was just being polite and cared nothing about her career, but she felt she must answer. As always, she leaped right in. "I'm a reporter for the *Boston Tribune*, Mrs. Curtis. I've always wanted to be a journalist, ever since high school in Denver when I used to help Dad with his Timberline Press. I have a column called 'Painting the Town,' which appears regularly, twice a week."

"That's wonderful, dear. Henry, remind me. We must start subscribing to the *Tribune* so we can read Andrea's column. But tell me, Andrea. Does that leave any time for volunteer work? I've always found working for the symphony so rewarding, and it's such a nice group of volunteers; women I've known forever."

"Andrea doesn't have time for that right now," interrupted Lowell. "But I'm sure she can make room for the Women's Symphony Committee sometime in the future."

Andy was pleased to have Lowell come to her rescue, but she felt vaguely disquieted at his offering of her services.

Mrs. Curtis reached over and took Andy's left hand. Andy's long, delicate fingers seemed enveloped in Mrs. Curtis's leathery ones. "Your ring is sweet, dear. Lowell tells me you didn't want to wear the one handed down from Grandmother Hopkins."

Andy looked to Lowell for support. His eyes were looking at the floor. "We, I mean, I just thought we wanted to have something that was just ours, I guess."

"Well, our family is strong on tradition. But no matter. That's what makes horse races. Isn't that so, Henry?"

Henry Curtis, pleased to be included in the conversation, took this as a cue to speak. "Of course. Now, Andrea, you and I must make some extra time together so I can show you my orchid collection in the greenhouse out back. I have some extremely rare varieties."

Andrea wondered if Mrs. Curtis ever went out to her husband's greenhouse or whether he used it as an escape. But then, Ben's ranch had been a refuge, too. It was there he hid from Grace's garden clubs and bridge luncheons. Andy liked Henry Curtis. She felt he was honest and steadfast. And probably unappreciated.

"I'd like to see your greenhouse, Mr. Curtis," said Andy. "I haven't had much time for flowers, but I'm willing to learn. Maybe it'd make an interesting story for my column."

Lowell, slouching in the wing chair, looked totally relaxed, but Andy could tell he was following the conversation intensely. "Andrea, darling," Lowell spoke up, "you must realize that the Curtises don't like to be written up in the papers. How does it go, Mother? 'One is in the papers only for birth, marriage, and death.'"

Andy was about to tell Lowell he was crazy. People made news, people made headlines. The public was entitled to know. She decided for once to keep quiet until they were alone. Margaret Curtis locked knowing eyes with her son as Maureen arrived with a silver platter covered with a lace doily and filled with watercress sandwiches. She offered the tray in silence.

Andy was starved. Her rushed day at the *Trib* had left no time for lunch. Although she wanted four, she said, "Thank you," and took only one.

"Speaking of marriage," said Mrs. Curtis, "and after all, that's why we're here, why don't you tell

THE BEST MAN

us what is going on. I know the wedding is up to the bride, but well, I have a few suggestions you may like. When Lowell was engaged to Nancy Phipps, both families were in accord on just everything."

Andy turned to Lowell. He had never mentioned Nancy Phipps before. He had told her about Janine, the Swiss banker's daughter he'd had a fling with in Paris, as well as other brief affairs—but no Nancy Phipps.

"She was ten years older. I just thought I was terribly sophisticated back then," said Lowell.

He'd passed off the explanation with a flick of his hand as he did anything that he considered unimportant. But what had happened? Who had broken off the engagement? And why? Andy's reporter's mind made her uneasy with this lack of important information.

"The wedding's going to be on June sixteenth, Mother. It will be at Trinity Church, of course. Andy consented to that when I told her how much it would mean to you."

"Thank you, dear," said Mrs. Curtis—to Lowell only, not to Andy. "Andrea, I do hope you'll let me do the flowers in the chuch. I guess Lowell must have told you. I've been head of the altar guild for about ten years now."

"Of course, Mrs. Curtis," answered Andy, who couldn't have cared less about the altar guild or the flowers.

"The groom's family always has the rehearsal dinner. I guess I'll use the Chilton Club."

"That's a bit stuffy, Mother. All those Irish biddies who can hardly stay afloat passing limp hors d'oeuvres."

Margaret Curtis laughed. "Oh, Lowell. You have the funniest way of putting things. I won't use the Chilton Club if you children don't want it."

Children! Andy was startled by the word. Lowell was an international banker. Andy was a reporter, totally self-supporting.

"Maybe you're right, Lowell. What about the Somerset?" Mrs. Curtis poured herself a third glass of sherry. Andy noticed her lined face was getting flushed.

"Mother, why don't we wait until both families get together to talk about those things?" said Lowell as he rose from the wing chair, stretched, and came over and sat between Andy and his mother on the couch.

"Just one little thought, Lowell. Have you sent the engagement announcements to the proper papers?"

Andy decided Margaret Curtis and Grace had a lot more in common than she'd first thought.

"Andrea is attending to that, Mother," said Lowell, squeezing Andy's hand. "That's her business, you know."

"Of course, I almost forgot."

"And she even made an appointment at Shreve's this coming Saturday to register for wedding presents."

"How efficient of you, dear," said Mrs. Curtis, obviously pleased with this activity. "I always say, ask a busy person, they're the ones who have the time."

Andy took the cliché as a compliment. She decided she'd spent enough time for the first encounter. Her head ached a little. She had to research a piece on facilities for the homeless. It was a far cry from the Chilton Club to bag ladies. She wondered if Lowell would understand her feelings of guilt, sitting in such splendor, about to write about the underprivileged.

Andy got up and Lowell followed her lead. "This has been wonderful, Mrs. Curtis. I can't wait until the family dinner when we iron out all the wedding plans. My mother is dying to meet you. And, Mr. Curtis, I do want to see that orchid collection." Andy smiled warmly at Henry Curtis. He came over and kissed her cheek.

"Lowell's chosen well," he said.

"Whatever Lowell wants is what we want for him," said Margaret Curtis.

"Thank you, Mother," said Lowell. "She likes you, Andrea," he whispered, "I can tell. Andrea, let's grab a bite at the Hungry i."

Andy felt tired and confused. A lot was happening here. She wanted time to sort it out. "Thanks, Lowell. But I think I'll take a cab home and grab a tuna sandwich. I have a lot of work to do. Why don't you stay here and have dinner with your family?"

"That would be a treat, Lowell. We hardly catch a glimpse of you these days," said Mrs. Curtis.

Lowell ushered Andy down the spiral staircase and out into the soft night air. "It would be a good night to be together, just you and me," he said.

"I know, it would be. But I can tell your family

wants to be with you. I don't blame them. Stay. Your mother will be in seventh heaven."

"Thanks for being so understanding, Andrea. I adore you. You're like no other girl I've ever had. Mother liked you, too. I could tell."

"I love you, Lowell. We—we just have a lot to talk about."

Lowell hailed a cab. Andy impulsively threw her arms around Lowell's neck, kissed him hard, and rode off into the night.

Her apartment on Linneaen Street seemed smaller and more anonymous than ever after the Beacon Hill town house, so crammed with possessions, with memories of the past. Andy decided that she must learn to appreciate material things more—the fine rugs, the chandeliers—since these things seemed to be a part of Lowell.

But, thought Andy, what about Margaret Curtis? She seemed charming and accepting, yet her adoration of Lowell worried Andy. It was almost as if Andy were breaking up a thirty-year love affair.

Andy decided to put all such musings out of her head and instead dreamed about the magical week at Stowe. That's what she wanted her life with Lowell to be like—at night and on weekends, anyway. He'd have his work during the day, and she'd be Pete Steiner's. She grabbed a tuna sandwich, wolfed it down, then set her alarm for five so she could get up and write her piece, jumped into bed, and fell fast asleep.

FIVE

Andy and Lowell sped along the Charles River in Lowell's Peugeot. Lowell liked his car. "Fast but not showy," he'd said. "And I'll always feel like I own a little bit of France."

A few sturdy sailors were braving the spring breezes, and college boys in large sculls were practicing for the May crew races.

"I never could understand that sport," said Andy. "Just pulling a paddle while some guy in front yells 'stroke and stroke and stroke.'"

"It's teamwork, darling. No arguments. Just doing what the boss says." Lowell's blue eyes sparkled, but his jaw protruded a bit as he sped in and out of the Memorial Drive traffic.

"That might be okay for crew racing but not for

us," said Andy. "In our life we're going to share and share alike. Make joint decisions."

Lowell looked so handsome in his blue blazer and oxford gray shirt that Andy decided not to pursue the subject. She really hadn't had a chance to talk to him about the Beacon Hill dinner. It had gone all right, she supposed, but something about it was vaguely unsettling. She couldn't put her finger on it, but something about the family dynamics and Lowell's attentions to his mother didn't quite jell with the independent international banker who had swept her off her feet after she'd crashed into that snow drift. Wasn't it funny the way one wrong twist had changed her life? One minute she was a career woman, missing her rural past but trying to put it behind her, and wham, along came this blond prince who'd whisked her into a whole new world. So much was happening, it took her breath away.

Andy never realized how much there was to getting married. Here they were, the two of them, already registering at Shreve's. Andy wished she'd had more time. They hadn't even talked about their tastes, but Andy knew from his family, and everything Lowell had indicated about himself, that he liked to stay with tradition. She, on the other hand, was a thoroughly modern Millie. Fancy china just wasn't high on her priority list. Amy and Mom would go right along with Lowell, of course. They both loved anything that hinted a good background—money, art, expensive possessions.

Andy's mind flashed to the Blue Ridge Ranch.

Ben and she had just come in from riding through the aspens. "Hey, girl. How about rustling me up some pan-fried potatoes and chili? I'll get out our best tin plates and mugs."

"Sure, Dad. You just boil some coffee. Don't forget to put some eggshells in." How could she ever tell Lowell about putting eggshells in boiled coffee?

As Lowell neared Back Bay, Andy took a deep breath and started in on the subject of the day—registering. "Lowell, I know it's nice to register for wedding presents, but we really haven't talked about it. I'm a little embarrassed. I'm sure the guys at the office have only heard about registering to vote or for the draft. I feel like a jerk picking out presents for them to give me."

"Andrea, everybody registers for wedding presents, at least everybody I know. It's just expected. I'm sure your mother has told you this."

Andy knew this activity was right up her mother's alley, to say nothing of Amy's.

"Mother registered at Shreve's when she married Daddy," Lowell continued, and I'm sure your mother did before she married your father and moved to Denver."

"Oh, I know she did," said Andy. "Uncle Simon insisted. He went with her, I think. Dad would have nothing to do with it. You're right about Mom, though. It took all my persuasive powers to keep her from coming with us. Amy even told me to turn every piece of china over and make sure it read bone. Honestly!"

"Andrea, you're going to be my wife, Mrs. Lowell Curtis, in less than two months. I think you can live through this. Come on, beautiful, make like it's fun."

"Lowell, I've covered Back Bay burglaries, muggings, kids selling coke in Brookline, but this is absolutely out of my league. I know the families want a big wedding, but my friends, well, they're just starting out, like I am. They can't afford big-deal presents."

"We'll pick out all sorts, Andrea. Just take it in stride. It's part of the deal. You can handle anything, Andrea. That's why I love you. Just wait till you're the wife of international banker Lowell Curtis, giving all those glamorous dinner parties."

Andy Ferguson giving glamorous dinner parties. Andy didn't picture her life that way. She'd never had time to organize the way Mom did. Why, that was a big part of Mom's life. Always had been. She was sure that's why Ben loved their ranch so much. Her pals from the *Trib* would be happy with spaghetti and meatballs. But what about Lowell's banker friends? Would they expect a big deal—shining crystal, polished silver? Who would have time to shine and polish?

"Just wait till you're the husband of Andy Ferguson, star reporter," she said.

"*Touché*, my pretty," said Lowell. There was no more time for conversation as he pulled into the Ritz parking lot.

"Let's not park here," said Andy. "It's highway robbery. We can park in the public parking under the Common for much less."

"You're absolutely right, star reporter. 'Waste not, want not,' my mother always says."

As they walked along Boylston Street, Andy looked into the windows of all the elegant stores. Emaciated mannequins in blue-and-white-checked spring suits. Wax male figures outfitted just like Lowell. This was definitely not familiar territory. "Mom used to bring Amy around here her senior year at Conn," said Andy, half to herself and half to Lowell. "That was after Uncle Simon died, and she inherited her nest egg."

Dad would certainly be astonished to see Mom now, back in Boston—just where she always wanted to be. Among, as she always said, "her people." But then, he'd be plenty amazed at what was happening to his favorite daughter. Not the *Trib* part. No, he'd like that. Especially knowing that his girl had a column of her own. And only twenty-six, too.

But Lowell. Andy tried to analyze what Ben would think of Lowell. She had thought about it a lot these past two months. His magnetic looks, his charm, his casual wit—Ben wouldn't care about that. No, he'd just care that all was well with his Andy, that Lowell had heart and intelligence, a will to succeed, and an ability to laugh at himself. Oh, it was all too confusing. That was Dad, all right, but was that Lowell? Of course it was. Stop brooding, Andy Ferguson. Full speed ahead.

"Your Dad never could make a go of that publishing house, could he?" said Lowell. "But you'll have nothing to worry about. I'll take care of you."

For a moment that felt good to Andy, being

taken care of, protected. That's what Dad used to do. But was this what she wanted now? She'd put the past to rest, hadn't she? But the future. Nope. That had to be even steven. She wanted an equal partnership—share and share alike.

"We'll take care of each other," said Andy firmly, as they approached the store so revered by generations of Bostonians.

A uniformed doorman ushered Andy and Lowell inside. Andy immediately unzipped her overstuffed black leather purse. "I'm going to take notes of everything," she said. As she pulled out her thick reporter's notebook, the purse, filled to overflowing, exploded. Onto the floor rolled a lipstick, a crumpled Kleenex, a pocket tape recorder, and a paperback dictionary. Mortified, she bent to scoop up her belongings. As she did, she felt a tickling sensation start at her ankle and slowly move up her trim leg. Damn. She had a run in her brand new white panty hose. Lowell looked in the other direction.

"Thanks for not teasing me," she said. He removed his hand from her grasp as a gray-haired woman, her ample bosom stuffed into a dark blue shirtwaist dress, approached.

"Good afternoon, sir. My name is Miss Mountain. May I be of help?"

Andy, uncomfortable in the first place, did not like the way she was being bypassed for Lowell. Would it always be like this? Lowell, so sure of himself, and Andy Ferguson, okay in the press room but a clod in society? Andy, stop being so hard on yourself. Lowell loves you. He says so all the time. He had done all the pursuing. Andy Ferguson would handle this old battleax.

"You may help both of us," said Andy a bit too strongly.

The Boston dowager, her hair pulled back in a bun, glared at Andy.

"We're going to be married," said Andy, "and we've come here to register."

"My family is the Curtis family," interjected Lowell. "We have patronized your store for generations. We've always used your services."

Lowell walked over to a glass case in the middle of the room. It was filled with delicate small boxes and vases. On the top of the cabinet was a delicate perfume flask of porcelain. Miss Mountain and Andy joined him.

"I'm honored to serve the Curtis family for yet another generation," said Miss Mountain.

"And the Fergusons, too," said Andy. "I'm Andy Ferguson."

As Andy thrust out her arm to shake Miss Mountain's hand, her shoulder-strap purse swung around to the right. With a whoosh, the porcelain container went crashing to the marble floor. It broke into tiny pieces. Andy looked at Lowell, aghast. Miss Mountain stiffened discernibly.

"I'm terribly sorry, Miss Mountain. I'll replace it, of course."

"Just send the bill to me at the First Shamut Bank," said Lowell.

"Lowell, this was my fault. I'll pay for it even if it takes a whole week's salary," said Andy. Then she smiled. Her wide grin lit up the room. "I'm just a bull in a china shop. I guess I'm better on assignments in the combat zone." Andy could see Lowell relax. Her unsophisticated approach, as always, touched him.

Miss Mountain cleared her throat. "Now, now. It was only a little mishap. Follow me to my office, and we'll fill out your card before we take a tour of the store."

Andy followed Miss Mountain gingerly through the myriad of glass cases filled with plates, cups, saucers, and silver. Lowell, three steps behind, brought up the rear.

"Come on, Lowell," said Andy, grabbing his arm and pulling him alongside her. "We're in this together. I'm not the Queen of England."

Lowell laughed.

Miss Mountain led Andy and Lowell to a small office at the end of the main floor. There was a leather-topped table in the center of the room, one chair on one side, two on the other. On the tabletop was a stack of manila files. The walls were covered with pictures of brides in wedding dresses and framed, printed wedding announcements from *The Boston Globe* and *The New York Times.* No *Trib* announcements here.

Her experienced, reportorial eye, able to read upside down, noted the names on the top file. *Nancy Weatherbee and Harold Logan, wedding date, June 25, 1988. Presents sent after June 24 to be addressed to Mr. and Mrs. Harold Logan, Jr.* Miss Mountain walked around the table, sat down, and pulled open a drawer. She pushed the other

THE BEST MAN

files aside and placed a fresh one on the faded leather top.

"Now," she said, "What is our wedding date?"

"June sixteenth," said Andy. Miss Mountain wrote both their names and then repeated, "Wedding date, June sixteenth. Presents to be sent after June fifteenth to be addressed to Mr. and Mrs. Lowell Curtis."

"Pardon me," said Andy. "May I see what you just wrote?"

"Why, of course," said Miss Mountain. She turned the file around.

"I'm sorry, Miss Mountain, but this is not correct."

"Oh, Miss Ferguson. Did I misspell your name? I'm glad you caught it. That would be simply dreadful."

"Oh, no. It's not that. Just cross out the Mr. and Mrs. I'm keeping my maiden name."

It was Lowell's turn to look surprised. He looked at her and lowered his voice. Andy knew he was angry. She'd listened to him lower his voice with others—on the phone in business conversations—but she'd never heard him lower his voice when he talked to her. She knew why. They just hadn't talked about her keeping the name Ferguson. There seemed to be so many things they hadn't talked about. Philosophies they hadn't exchanged. She just never seemed to have enough time. It was always tennis, movies, romantic dinners, and then making love, but not time enough to just talk, explore each other's minds. No, they hadn't done that, and still Andy instinctively knew

Lowell would want her to take the name Curtis. And she knew she wasn't about to.

"Andrea," said Lowell, with his voice lowered. "You and I haven't talked about this."

"I know, Lowell. But please understand. I've been Andrea Ferguson for twenty-six years, and I plan to stay that way for the next twenty-six. Gloria Steinem has not lived in vain."

"We'll talk about this later," said Lowell. "I guess I'm just a bit out of sync with the women's movement. How will I ever explain this to Mother?"

Andy was grateful for Miss Mountain's interruption.

"Ahem." She fluttered as she reached in her folder and produced a typed list. "Here's what my store recommends for today's bride and groom."

Andy noticed there were many typewritten pages. "But we won't have space for too much. We're looking for a small apartment in Cambridge."

Lowell winked at Miss Mountain. Andy felt the two of them were in cahoots. "That's just for a little while until our family starts growing."

Andy felt as if someone had kicked her in the stomach. They had never discussed children at all and here was Lowell, talking about his growing family to an absolute stranger. He seemed so happy, though. His eyes were shining. After all, there would be little Curtises someday. It was just a question of when. Nothing that couldn't be worked out.

"Mother and Daddy will store the overflow,"

said Lowell. "That is, if your mother doesn't want to. I don't know how much room she has for storage in that ranch house in Newton."

"More than we'll ever need," said Andy breezily. "Now, let's get on with this. I have to be home by five. Pete's calling me with a new assignment."

"He calls you on Saturday with a new assignment?"

Lowell was right. Pete never called her on Saturdays. But this was supposed to be something special. "I don't know any more than you do, but we just better be back at Linneaen by five."

"Fine," said Lowell. "Let's get started."

"Of course, of course," clucked Miss Mountain. "I suppose you want to start with your flat silver."

"Fine with me," said Lowell. "I've always had a yen for Aunt Pru's pattern. Mother told me it's Kirk Stieff's Repoussé."

"Why do we need flat silver at all? I'll never have time to polish it."

"It's now or never, Miz Wiz," said Lowell. "This is the only time Mother's pals kick in, so we might as well take advantage of it. Every Shreve's baby is born with a silver spoon in his mouth."

"Oh, Miss Ferguson. You do have an amusing fiancé, if you don't mind my saying so," chortled Miss Mountain.

Andy decided she'd better not bring up stainless steel. It was a losing battle. She'd just have to go buy some herself.

Miss Mountain showed Andy and Lowell the displays of bibelots, vases, clocks, and plates, then led them through an imposing archway, into a room of floor-to-ceiling shelves loaded with silver trays, pitchers, and martini shakers. On a large, semicircular table covered with black velvet were placed knives, forks, and spoons in varied patterns. Miss Mountain brightened up considerably.

"Well, here we are, my dears. Whatever you pick you'll be eating on the rest of your lives, as will your children and their children in generations to come. We've arranged each pattern by place settings. Luncheon, dinner, and salad forks, luncheon and dinner knives, dessert and cream soup spoons. Not everybody includes the iced teas."

"That's an awful lot of knives and forks," Andy said. "You can only eat with one at a time."

"I don't think we'll pick out a luncheon set, Miss Mountain," said Lowell with a smile. "Miss Ferguson and I will just go for the dinner set."

Walking over to the table, Lowell picked up a heavy fork. The handle was covered with small roses. "Why, here's Aunt Pru's pattern," he said. "How much is a knife, fork, and spoon of this?"

"That's the Kirk Stieff Repoussé you mentioned earlier. A five-piece place setting is two hundred eighty-six dollars," said Miss Mountain.

"Lowell, that's wild."

"I agree, Andrea."

"And it's just too fancy. I remember when we lived in Denver Mom used to take her silver out of a big wooden box just for Thanksgiving and Christmas. The pattern was perfectly simple. Just a scallop on the edge. It meant a lot to her, so Dad never said anything. The rest of the time we just used stainless and it was fine. I like it better than

any of this stuff. It's cheaper and it's practical."
There, she said it, and she was glad.

"Andy, dear. Giving dinner parties isn't practical. It's a banker's way of life."

Amy would love all this. Grace would, too. She would have loved "a banker's way of life." Andy wasn't sure she could ever preside over dinner parties. "Isn't there anything else, Miss Mountain?"

"Well, we do handle Christofle. It's nickeled silver, not sterling, but a lot of our modern busy brides are picking it out. No insurance to pay because it can't be melted down, and it does beautifully in a dishwasher. The Vendôme has a simple shell at the bottom. Like the pattern you were describing, which your mother used for the holidays. It's French, you know, so the back part is decorated. Napoleon used it. It's less, of course. One hundred sixty-five per setting."

French! Andy knew that Lowell would be pleased. "Oh, Lowell. That sounds so much better. Besides, I just can't see myself rushing home from a hot story at six, and pulling out the silver to polish while I nuke frozen chicken breasts in the microwave." Andy's face brightened. "Now there's something I really want. Where's your microwave department?"

"We don't have such items here," said Miss Mountain. "Our store started in 1800. I'm certain Mr. Curtis's grandmother's engagement ring was bought here." Andy fingered the simple engagement ring she had picked out with Lowell. The one she wanted. She knew Lowell would have much preferred her to have his grandmother's. Not that it was showy. It was just that it was in the family. But they were starting off fresh.

Lowell had told her hundreds of times he was bringing some new blood into the Curtis family. He'd said she was different from anybody else he'd ever known, and that's why he adored her. So the ring should be theirs and theirs alone. Grandmother's could wait. Lowell gazed longingly at Andy. She shivered ever so slightly. Everything was going to be all right.

"My grandmother's ring did indeed come from here, Miss Mountain," said Lowell. "I'm saving it for our twentieth."

"How sweet," said Miss Mountain, her bosom heaving slightly. "Now we'd better continue. Miss Ferguson says she has to be home by five, and that only gives us a few hours."

"That's more time than it took me to interview that weirdo who broke into the Channel Five newsroom and tried to grab the mike," Andy whispered to Lowell.

He playfully smacked her bottom and smiled. "What's next, Miss Mountain?"

Miss Mountain preened herself. "Well, we'd better do the china." As Andy and Lowell followed her around the showcase, Lowell stopped in front of an open closet filled with glasses. He picked up a tumbler with a tennis player etched on it. "Oh, I'll mark those down," said Miss Mountain. "They come in sets of twelve. Highball and old-fashioned. Thirty-five dollars a dozen. Quite reasonable—a bargain."

"That's a good idea," said Andy. "We both like tennis, and they're not too expensive."

"Oh, we have exquisite Baccarat, too," said Miss Mountain. "Though some of our brides prefer Waterford."

Andy turned to Lowell. "No Baccarat, for heaven's sake. Or Waterford, either. You know me. I'd break it in a minute. Dad had jelly glasses on the ranch, and we'd even bust those. Let's go look at china."

Miss Mountain took them around the corner to a separate area where tables were set. Each arrangement displayed a set of silver, a wineglass, water goblet, and china, all of different styles and patterns. In the middle of each plate, in a silver card holder, was the name of the bride and groom who'd selected them.

"We'll be making up one of these for you soon," beamed Miss Mountain, finally in her element. She pointed beyond the table to cupboards of plates, cups, and saucers. "This is a very popular pattern with our brides. The gold rim around the white plate is elegant. Helena Cosgrove chose it, and so did Elizabeth Painter. Elizabeth was filling out a set that had belonged to her mother, I believe."

Andy toyed with her soft, curly hair. Why did everything have to be so formal? So forbidding. This wasn't her lifestyle. Lowell seemed to enjoy informality, too ... except when he was on Beacon Hill, of course. But even with all his worldliness, he seemed to relish kicking off his shoes. She hadn't been able to recapture the spontaneity of their week in Stowe, but this had been a hectic two months for both of them. She hadn't planned on this humongous wedding at all. Lowell must understand how pressured she felt.

Lowell cleared his throat. "Miss Mountain," he said. "I think my fiancée and I would prefer a pattern a little more lively. Perhaps a Spode, like the one over there with the blue flowers."

Andy looked at the Spode. A bit too Laura Ashley. But how not to hurt Lowell's feelings. He'd been defending her all afternoon. "Lowell," she said, "that is more homey, but honestly, I'd be happy with something more contemporary." Andy fingered a Villeroy and Bach plate.

"That's the basket-weave pattern. It's one hundred and twelve dollars and fifty cents for dinner, salad, bread and butter, and cup and saucer."

"Wow. Don't you have anything for less."

"This is new," said Miss Mountain. "A little too new for my taste, but everybody's different." She pointed to a white porcelain plate with a black square border.

"Oh," said Andy. "I like that. Is it a king's ransom, too?"

"That's Metropolis Black by Sasaki. Thirty-two a place setting."

"Miss Mountain, I think we've got it," said Lowell.

Andy, so thankful they were in agreement, added, "Miss Mountain, if anybody really wants to, they can give us that Spode Canterbury tea set." Maybe she would have Aunt Pru someday for tea. Maybe, just once.

Miss Mountain wrote *Sasaki, Metropolis Black*

beside *china pattern*. This job completed, she said, "Now, Miss Ferguson and Mr. Curtis, here comes the fun time. How many guests have you included for your big event?"

"Two hundred and fifty or thereabouts," said Lowell.

That seemed to please Lowell and the Curtises, thought Andy. Certainly Mom wanted it that way. But what about me, Andy Ferguson? I'm Ben Ferguson's daughter, too. But he's not here, or I'd be getting married by a preacher at the ranch. I wonder how Lowell would take it. But that's all behind me. Come on, Ms. Andrea Ferguson. It's on to Trinity Church.

"The perfect size," interjected Miss Mountain. "Now you two can relax. Wander through our store and anything your hearts desire, just tell me, and I'll put it on your list. Remember, it's only once in a lifetime."

Andy pulled Lowell aside. They stood by a glass vase filled with seashells. It had been made into a lamp. She had to make him understand her feelings. "Lowell," she said, "I know that Mom and Amy would love to be doing this and your parents think it's what's expected of me, but I think it's, well, presumptuous."

Andy envisioned Pete and Gabe slouching into Shreve's in their rumpled trenchcoats. "Now, Miss Mountain," Pete would say. "Andy Ferguson said I could come in here and pick out a wedding present for her. How about that little box over there? That's kinda nice."

"Of course, sir," Miss Mountain would click.

"That's an old snuff box. A Battersea box. A charming keepsake."

"How much?" Pete would say. "Three hundred and fifty dollars," Miss Mountain would say?

Andy was becoming agitated. Her face was rosy, her eyes glistening. Lowell approached and gently put an arm around her trim waist. "Andrea," he said. "You do look lovely when you're angry, but that doesn't help the situation. This is something your mother wants you to do. Mother and Daddy expect it of me, too. It's just a custom. Let's finish up and enjoy."

There was Lowell, taking over again. He seemed to be manipulating her. No, that was too harsh a word. He was thinking about her, sure he was. He just wanted to appease everyone. Not a bad idea. Andy didn't want unpleasantness. "You're right, Lowell," she said. "Where are your less expensive gifts, Miss Mountain?"

"Why, right over there in our little gift shop."

Andy and Lowell, trailed by Miss Mountain, left the Battersea boxes and silver toast racks. They headed through a hall to the immediate right of the entrance. Over a mahogany door, a wooden painted sign said GIFT SHOP. Inside were wicker baskets, green-and-yellow plastic picnic plates, and Lucite trays in all sizes.

"I feel better already," said Andy.

Lowell picked up some hunter-green washable place mats with tennis rackets and gold clubs forming a border. "Now, here's something practical you'll like, Miss Andrea Ferguson."

Andy decided this was not the time or place to

point out she was Ms. Ferguson. "Lowell, the mats are fine but I think they'll look pretty silly on that old card table Mom's lending us."

"We won't be dining that way too long," said Lowell.

"Well, I should hope not," said a familiar voice in the doorway. Andy wheeled around to see Amy. She was wearing a light blue jersey spring suit. A big white-and-blue polka-dot bow peeked out of the bolero jacket. Her blond, wavy hair swept softly over her shoulders.

"Amy Ferguson, what are you doing here?" said Andy.

"I just happened to be window-shopping on Boylston Street and decided to pop in." Three inches shorter than her sister, Amy looked up, pale blue eyes wide and innocent.

"Nonsense, Amy. Mom told you we were going to be here. Besides, this is just your cup of tea." It was just like Amy. Butting in, always competing for the attention of Andy's boyfriends. Amy gazed at Lowell, who seemed genuinely pleased at her arrival.

"Hi." Amy offered Lowell her hand. "I don't think we've met. I'm Andrea's baby sister. I just came to see what you two had picked out. Kind of a rehearsal for when *my* big moment comes."

Miss Mountain, thrilled to help, said, "Why, Miss Ferguson picked out Sasaki. She likes contemporary. Though I think I've talked them into a Spode tea service. Mr. Curtis said his grandmother had one."

"Oh," said Amy. "I love Spode anything. You remember Tina, don't you, Andy?"

How could Andy forget Tina? Amy and Tina had spent the night in the Beta house at Trinity instead of registering for classes at Conn College. Andy had been horrified. The first day of college and Amy was already goofing off.

"Well," said Amy, "She picked out Spode Tearose. She had the most fa-abulous do. Five hundred under a pink tent in Newport with Peter Duchin playing. Lowell, why don't you show me all the loot you picked out? You must have had a ball."

"We've pretty much covered the first floor," said Lowell. "Everything we picked out is in good taste, due as much to Miss Mountain here as to us." Lowell cocked his head toward Miss Mountain, who beamed.

That's Lowell, thought Andy. He always makes someone feel important when he can use them. No, Andy, she scolded herself. That's unfair. Lowell's just good at handling people.

"It's such a pleasure working with the Curtis family, and I'm honored to meet the younger Miss Ferguson. I hope someday we can be of service to you."

"I can hardly wait," said Amy. "Now, come on. I want to see the antiques. I can always use them in my interior decorating."

"What antiques?" said Andy.

"Why, the whole second floor is antiques. Haven't you been there?"

"I really don't have much time, Amy. I have to be home for a phone call in forty-five minutes."

"Oh, let's give it a whirl," said Amy. "You may never be back here."

Amy led Andy and Lowell up the staircase in the middle of the room, followed by a huffing Miss Mountain.

"This floor is more for the bride's first home than her first apartment," said Miss Mountain. "For after she's settled down to be a wife and mother."

Arguing with Miss Mountain was useless, so Andy decided to keep mum and let Amy and Miss Mountain have their day.

"Look at those lovely tin urns," said Amy.

"Mother has some on Beacon Hill," said Lowell. "They're English chestnut urns."

"They're beautiful," said Amy, gazing at Lowell. "You know, I've never been in your family's house, and yet I know exactly what it's like. I can't wait until our families get together and I meet your parents."

Andy looked at Amy. So pert. So poised. Always saying the right thing. She was glad the registering was coming to an end. She pushed back her cuff and looked at her Timex watch.

"Lowell, we just have to go. I have to be home by five and it's already four-fifteen. If Pete calls and hears my machine say, 'Hello, you've reached . . . ,' he'll hang up and maybe even give my assignment to Gabe."

Lowell put out his hand and firmly shook Miss

Mountain's. "It's been wonderful working with you."

"Thank you, Mr. Curtis," purred Miss Mountain. "I'll have the list Xeroxed and copies sent to you and to Miss Ferguson. We'll also have one in the files so the clerks can check off the items as they're purchased. Now, do you want to go over the list?"

"Oh, I'm afraid we don't have time for that," said Andy. "But I know you'll handle it perfectly. Come on, Lowell." Andy darted down the staircase. " 'Bye, Amy. We're going to have a big family powwow next week to discuss all the plans. See you then."

Amy blew Lowell a kiss as he ran down the stairs after Andy. "I just love being a part of all this."

"Step on the gas, Lowell. We haven't much time," said Andy as Lowell snaked in and out of the Boston traffic. At last they were whizzing across the Lars Anderson Bridge toward Linneaen Street. Andy looked at Lowell. His light hair was slightly mussed, but otherwise he was his impeccable self. Imperturbable, too. It seemed the registration ordeal hadn't bothered him at all. Maybe he enjoyed it.

"Did you fasten your seat belt, Andrea?"

"I always seem to forget that. This time my excuse is I'm too excited about my next assignment. You know, Lowell. Pete might seem like a grouch sometimes, but he's a first-rate editor and a teddy bear."

Lowell frowned at that, and Andy was curious

about his mood change. "What's the matter, Mr. International Banker?"

"It's just that you seem twice as excited about your new assignment as all those wedding presents we're going to get."

"I admit I'm more interested in a hot story than a silver pickle fork. Wouldn't you be more stimulated by finding some undeveloped real estate for a Dutch client than an afternoon at Shreve's?"

"Apples and oranges, Andrea. You can't compare them."

Andy wished Lowell would answer her directly. Figuring out what was going on in his head was so difficult sometimes.

They remained silent as the Peugeot fought its way through Harvard Square to Linneaen Street. Lowell pulled up to her building. Green paint was peeling off the shutters of the undistinguished brick apartment house. Andy had never cared. She wondered if Lowell did. She jumped out of the car. "Hope you can find a place to park, sweetheart. I'd better run."

Andy darted up the steps and fumbled for the keys. Once inside, she sprawled on the brown tweed couch and kicked off her pumps. The heels were too high, anyway. She was much more comfortable in flats. Her digital clock flashed 4:47. Andy looked at the white phone on her maple table and the attached answering machine. No red light, no messages, and the phone wasn't ringing.

Lowell's knock sounded on her door the very moment the phone started to ring. She leaped across the room, opened the door, and was back in two jumps.

"Hello."

"Hello, Andy. Pete here."

"Hi, Pete," said Andy as she motioned Lowell to sit down on the couch. "There must be something big going up for you to schedule a Saturday call." Andy's voice was calm and professional. She was as self-assured here as she was self-conscious in the china department.

"Well, Ms. Ferguson. I've got some good news for you and some bad news."

She hoped Lowell would refer to her as *Ms.* instead of *Mrs.* someday.

"Bad news first please, Pete."

"Okay, gorgeous. Bad news is you're going to have to spend less time with your fancy boyfriend the next few weeks."

Andy didn't comment. "What's the good news, Pete?"

"Well, you know I've been working all week lining up the troops to cover Tom Bradford's campaign."

"Hell, I know," said Andy. "I'm damned annoyed that I didn't get a piece of the action."

Lowell sat on the couch with his hands crossed. He had never heard Andy speak this way.

"Well," said Pete, "I've looked over the copy and what's missing is human interest. We know the guy's big in ecology and conservation. He's given numerous speeches about the national seashore. He has a hell of an idea about using the abandoned Air Force base on the Lower Cape for low-rent housing for the elderly. But I don't think we have any idea what makes him tick."

"You mean his family tree? Where he prepped? C'mon, Pete, that's sob-sister stuff."

"No, gorgeous. I don't mean that at all. I want to know where he got his ideas. What kind of people he likes. Who his friends are. Where he eats. I want you to live and breathe Tom Bradford until you know his every thought. That would go over big with the readers, and I figure you're just the one who can do it."

Andy looked at Lowell and felt a pang, but only a slight one. "I think I should level with you, Pete. These next two months will be pretty hectic for me. I would only want to do this if I could give it my best shot."

"Your decision, lady."

Andy paused. She looked at Lowell and then back to the phone. "Okay, Pete," she said. "You're on."

SIX

Tom Bradford's small co-op overlooking the Charles River served as a bedroom and office in his fledgling campaign for the U.S. House of Representatives. "May have to expand," he often said, "but let's play it as it goes."

His young assistant, Chip Bowman, was reading the latest water-table statistics from the *Lower Cape Bulletin*. "It looks bad, Tom. They keep building those large condos around P-Town and the sewage problem is getting out of hand. The fishing areas are already endangered, and soon it'll be the beaches. They're using half of Truro's water, as it is. The wells can't take it forever."

"Yes, I know," said Tom. "I'm going to use that in my next speech. Have we got time to get at it now?"

"Sure thing, only don't forget that reporter, what's his name, has you from two to three."

"Oh yeah, that Ferguson guy, Andy. He's supposed to hype my image from cold and austere to charming and gallant. Not my style, but I guess it's necessary. When's he due?"

"About five minutes from now. Better put on a tie and comb your hair. Image, man, image!"

Tom Bradford wished he hadn't agreed to this foolishness. Almost on the hour, the bell rang.

"Come in," shouted Tom. "Chip, let him in and then grab yourself some lunch. I don't need you for this."

Andy, wearing a large poncho to ward off the late-April rain, stepped into the office, smiled, and extended her hand. "Hi, I'm Andy Ferguson."

That now-familiar look of confusion appeared on Tom's face. She secretly enjoyed the confusion her name evoked. But would he? Tom Bradford stared for a moment, then suggested Andy hang up her "rain thing" so they could get to work.

"Would you like some coffee?" he asked.

"Oh sure. I'd love some."

While Tom boiled water for instant, she stared out at the gray Charles River.

"This must be lovely on a sunny day. It's not far from the club where I play tennis."

"The Cambridge Tennis Club? I hear there's a five-year waiting list, not to mention pretty hefty dues."

"Oh, I'm only a guest," she said, a bit flustered. She never discussed her personal life in an interview.

"Oh, I see." He smiled.

"Milk and sugar?"

"No, black, please." She smiled back. "Now," she said, more seriously, "many people feel that you have a good chance against Gene Sorley. But so far he's garnered all the publicity, good and bad, and you know what they say about that?"

"Yeah. Any publicity's good."

"Exactly. The *Trib* is interested in the issues. And you've made yourself clear on them. By the way, you've done a terrific job exposing Sorley's conflict-of-interest deal with that Wareham consortium. But we want more coverage of the personal side of you. We have more than enough on your opponent. Every photo of Gene Sorley has him smiling with his arm around his wife or one of his five kids. He's always kissing a baby or Miss Massachusetts. His big cookouts are famous, and everyone goes. I even made it to one. The lobster was great."

Tom looked visibly darker. "I hate to think all that's so important."

"Well, it is—that is, if you want to get elected. Now, what I want is background. Too bad you're not married. That always helps. But I understand that your family has been on the Cape for generations. Weren't there some whalers and clipper-ship captains? That would help."

"Yes, they'd probably bust out of their graves if they knew I was going to exploit them, but you're right. I can see it's important. Bradfords, Macys, and Nickersons were all in whaling and china

THE BEST MAN 105

trade. You should see the fantastic screens and porcelains in some of the old Cape houses."

"What about Windswept?" asked Andy. "I read somewhere that you keep the old family place in Truro and plan to live there full time someday."

There was a change in Tom's expression. The rather harsh lines of his face seemed to fade. "Yes, it's always been the best place I know. I only wish I had more time to spend there. It needs fixing badly, especially the back porch, but the view is terrific. From the upstairs bedrooms you can always watch the sea. I wish you could—well, anyway, I go up there to walk and fish and straighten out my priorities. I get some of my best speeches done when I'm walking along the dunes or in the woods. But, hell, I don't want to sound like some Thoreau character. Isn't that what we want to avoid?"

"Not entirely," she said, then paused to observe him. He did have that loner look, she thought. And somebody ought to do something about his clothes. They looked slept in. The face was good, honest-looking. A little too serious, maybe. The hair was too long, and needed a trim on the sides. But his eyes were fine. He needed some good publicity shots. Well, she brought her Leica.

Tom, meanwhile, was looking at her more keenly. A glance at her knees provoked an unexpected fantasy of naked legs, a lithe torso, tousled hair, and warm gray eyes, all open to the sea, to him. Get a hold of yourself, Tom, he chided himself. This is business.

"Would you mind if I take a couple of head

shots?" she asked. "There aren't any in our files. If they come out all right, I'll have them blown up. Maybe next time you could get a haircut."

"Well, why not?" he laughed. "And next time you can bring some makeup, too."

"That won't be necessary," she said briskly. "Now, while I'm setting the focus, you can straighten your tie." Andy peered into the lens a long moment. Yes, he had possibilities: A rugged-looking face, beautiful eyes. Black or dark brown? They changed when he laughed. Almost black hair. Skin was a little pale. Needed some sun.

"You look too stiff," she said. "This isn't for posterity. Just keep talking, and I'll decide when to shoot."

"Okay," he smiled. "What shall I talk about? Fishing rights? Uh—what about meeting me for dinner some night?" Why was he saying this? She'd think he was on the make. As he thought more about it, maybe he was. There was something special about her. Her smile, her intelligence, a real woman . . . and those eyes. He smiled again.

Click!

"No time for dalliance," she quipped. Was that disappointment she saw? Was he serious? "Maybe lunch sometime."

He grinned. Click.

"I guess that'll do," she said. "Sure, I suppose I could do a lunchtime interview. Find out what the candidate eats."

"That's a great idea. I hate taking time from work."

"Isn't that part of the job?" she asked.

"Well, I guess it's going to have to be. I need all the help I can get to defeat that con man Sorley. How about The Harvest? It's right near here." Was she blushing?

"Uh, no," she said. "It's too crowded." Oh heck, why should she care where they met? "Well, sure. The Harvest will do fine. Let's see. How about Tuesday at one-thirty? Maybe you can get a table in the back." She hurriedly packed her gear and strode to the door.

"I'll be looking forward to that, Miss Ferguson," he said.

She was sure he meant it.

Five days after Andy'd first met with Tom Bradford, she still couldn't get him out of her mind. She knew he was a better candidate than Sorley. He had to win. He had all the right instincts. He didn't have the machine or the money that the Sorley group had, but he had charisma. That was for sure. Maybe her articles in the *Trib* would help. If he won, maybe she could always think it was in some small way due to her.

But there was no time to plan those articles today because tonight was the summit meeting at Beacon Hill. Mom, Amy, and the Curtises would all assemble to discuss wedding plans.

Andy assumed Roby wouldn't be there. Strange, Lowell hadn't talked about him since Stowe. His parents had never mentioned his name, either. Oh, well, lots of families have skeletons, and Lowell was her guy. The man of her dreams. The man with whom she'd spend the rest of her life.

Once they were married, everything would be fine. It was just all these wedding discussions that made her feel so uncomfortable and out of control. Better shape up, Ms. Andy Ferguson, today was Tuesday . . . Tuesday.

What else was today? She reached into her memory and suddenly realized that this was the day she was supposed to have a working lunch with Tom. But if she did, she wouldn't have time to get everything else done for the Curtises as well as complete her column by the five-o'clock deadline. Her personal life was interfering with her career. This couldn't keep happening. Oh, nuts. Andy flipped through her Rolodex and found the number for the Bradford office.

"Hello. Bradford for Congress."

"Hi, this is Andy Ferguson. May I please speak to Tom Bradford."

"This is Chip Bowman. I'm afraid Tom is tied up right now. Can I help you?"

"Tom and I were supposed to have lunch today to start a series of interviews."

"Yep. That's right here on his calendar."

"Well, I'm awfully sorry. I have to change the date. Can we make it tomorrow?"

"Let's see. No. I'm sorry. He's got Wednesday penciled out. Then he's going down to the Cape for the weekend. Do you want to try for next week?"

"Thanks, Chip, I'll get back to you. I feel dreadful about this." She really did—and not just on a professional level. That surprised her.

"We need all the publicity we can get, so do call next week, Ms. Ferguson."

"I will. That's for sure."

She would never cancel an interview again. Never. She wondered if it were subconsciously something about meeting Tom at The Harvest that bothered her. Ridiculous. Tom was business. Just because she and Lowell ate there had nothing to do with it. "Now, Andy Ferguson," she told herself, "on with the day. You messed up—once is okay but never again. From now on, wedding or no wedding, business before pleasure."

It was four-thirty when her final sentence for "Painting the Town" flashed on her computer screen. . . . *and that's what's new in Boston this week. Don't forget the Liz Harris Gallery. Harris brings the refreshing perspective of black American artists to New England.*

The plans for the dinner were set in stone. Grace and Amy would pick Andy up at seven. Lowell would meet them all on Chestnut Street. Drinks at seven-thirty, dinner at eight. Andy was running late and was hurriedly dressing.

Around her slim waist she hooked a new salmon silk skirt, then tucked in an écru tailored blouse. She unwrapped a new pair of panty hose—Teasingly Taupe—the color was all wrong. Oh, well. Nobody on Chestnut Street was going to notice the color of her stockings. Or her legs at all, for that matter . . . except Lowell.

Her Mom would be in seventh heaven tonight,

Andy thought as she ran down the four flights of stairs at seven. This would be Grace's shining hour. Amy would enjoy herself, too.

Grace's white four-door Cutlass was just pulling up when Andy hit the street. Amy was wearing a navy blue, skintight, V-neck, shows-all dress. Grace was in navy blue, too, with a soft white organza collar. They looked more like sisters than mother and daughter. Oddly, Andy did not feel a part of them. Just a catalyst for the evening.

"Where will we park, dear?" asked Grace as they approached the Curtis home. "You've been to Beacon Hill more recently than I have, although I did have dinner at the Lamsons's soon after my return here. Amy, we must remember to put them on the list."

"Mom, I hardly know the Lamsons, and I'm sure Lowell doesn't."

"You won't know all the Curtises' friends, either, darling. But they'll all mix just beautifully. You'll see."

"Mom, I—"

"Let's not argue on this exciting night."

"There's Lowell," exclaimed Amy, pointing to the handsome figure in front of the Curtis house. "Doesn't he look gorgeous? I'll bet he has some cute friends."

"Amy," said Grace, "Lowell is Andy's fiancé. And this is her evening. Remember. Your time will come."

Andy looked at Lowell, standing so princely and serene in front of the green door with the lion knocker. He looked so in command right then that

THE BEST MAN

she felt magnetically drawn to him. She just wished the whole commotion were over and they were alone together, just like they'd been in Stowe. But on with the show. This was Fergusons-meet-Curtises time.

Lowell leaned into the car. "Hello, Mrs. Ferguson, or rather, Hello, Grace. I do hope I can call you Grace. The family's really looking forward to this evening. And, Amy, you're even prettier than I remembered.

"Pull right in there. Parking's impossible here on the Hill, but Mother arranged with the Thompsons that you could have their spot. They'll be out for the evening. It's the Gardner Museum annual fund-raiser and the Hill's practically empty."

Lowell gave a mocking low bow as he pointed the way to the door. No Maureen opened the hallowed portal this time, but rather Mrs. Curtis herself, draped in a pallid silk chiffon dress. Mr. Curtis stood beside her, and Andy realized again how his wife towered over him. She wondered if they ever danced together. The image amused her.

"Hello, Andrea," said Mrs. Curtis, smiling her proper but emotionless smile. "How charming to see you again."

"Hello, Mrs. Curtis," said Andy. Lowell's mother had never told her to call her Margaret, and Andy—never as socially assured as Lowell—didn't attempt to. "This is my mother, Grace Curtis, and my sister, Amy."

"Do come in," said Henry Curtis. "We want to get to know you so we can all be one big, happy family."

Grace swept in, quite regally. Amy bounced beside her, almost skipping. They both seemed much happier to be there than Andy. Andy studied the group as Maureen stepped in to take coats. Grace, Amy, the Curtises, and Lowell all seemed united by one cause—planning the wedding. Why did she feel like an outsider here? It was *her* wedding. She walked over to Lowell, hoping to grab his hand for support, but he was busy making amenities and lightly brushed her off.

"Come on upstairs, everybody. Mother and I felt this occasion called for a bit of the bubbly, so let's all go upstairs and toast the wedding."

Mrs. Curtis led the way up the spiral stairs to the living room Andy remembered so well from her first meeting. That was only two weeks ago and yet so much had happened in Andy's professional life: her first big break into political reporting; meeting Tom Bradford. She liked and respected Tom. She knew what he stood for, what he was all about, and she was determined to do a good job on the interviews.

But what about Lowell? Andy wished the engagement party and wedding were over and the two of them were getting on with their lives. She hated showy occasions and small talk. But she knew how important all the formalities were to her mother, and how much tradition meant to Lowell and his mother. It was a family time, and she might as well try to please them all.

The lights were low in the living room. The Lalique chandelier glistened, reflecting in the French doors, darkened by nightfall. The faded green vel vet couch was softened by the artificial light. On the oriental coffee table was a silver tray, six fluted glasses and a bottle of Taittinger. For the first time, Andy noticed silver-framed family pictures on the black concert grand. There was Mrs. Curtis in her wedding dress, as tall and formidable as she was today, her hair blond like Lowell's. Henry Curtis, smiling beside her in his cutaway, looked pleased with the world. There were several pictures of Lowell: Lowell sailing, Lowell laughing on a ski slope, Lowell tall and preppy in his tennis whites. But it was another picture that caught Andy's well-trained eye. It was a photograph of the Curtises on a picnic in a field somewhere. There was an umbrella set up, a tablecloth, a wicker hamper, Mr. Curtis in Bermuda shorts, Mrs. Curtis in a flowered cotton skirt and large straw hat, Lowell in shorts and a T-shirt. The three of them were laughing together. On the fringe of the family was a smaller boy. Extremely thin and wearing blue jeans, he somehow did not seem to belong with the other three. Andy stopped short. That must be Roby.

"Come on, Andrea, join the fun," said Grace, who was obviously in her element. "Mrs. Curtis and I have discovered a mutual friend. Nancy Tibbs. You remember my talking about Nancy, my dear friend from Newton who went to Foxcroft?" Andy indeed remembered her mother's talking about her high-school chum whom Ben always referred to as Fancy Nancy. "What a small world this is, indeed," Grace was saying. "That we both should know Nancy Tibbs. Why, she was my very best friend for years." Andy cringed inwardly. Grace was overdoing it. Mrs. Curtis seemed uncomfortable. Andy looked at Lowell, who seemed to be delighted with Amy's attention.

"I knew loads of girls at Conn," he was saying. "They sure turn 'em out pretty. My friend Skip owns a pub here, The Beachcomber, and those Conn gals seem to gravitate there on the weekends."

"Oh, I've never been to The Beachcomber," said Amy. "I hear it's a blast. Andrea Ferguson, you sure are a lucky duck."

Andy had never been to The Beachcomber, either, and was certain the place wasn't her scene. After the wedding, she looked forward to being a couch potato, just she and Lowell, alone in their pad with some takeout moo goo gai pan. She walked over to Henry Curtis, who stood beside the coffee table, watching Mrs. Curtis politely endure the effervescent Grace.

"I do hope we have time when all this hoopla is over for me to see your orchid collection," Andy said softly.

"Anytime, Andrea. It would be my pleasure."

Lowell moved toward Andy and the champagne. She recognized his body language. He was about to take over.

"Come on, everybody. It's time to toast my beautiful bride. It will be the first of many toasts she'll receive. Not only during this wedding period, but during our long and fruitful life together."

"Oh, Lowell. You always say things better than anybody," purred Mrs. Curtis.

Andy said nothing. The words "my beautiful bride" bothered her. He made it sound as if he owned her. But he didn't—they were two individuals who were planning a wedding. They were equals, although Andy didn't feel so equal right now. She watched as Lowell twisted the top of the Taittinger.

"The secret is to have the cork just fall off quietly. Only a neophyte would try to shoot the cork across the room."

"I never knew that," cooed Amy. "Andrea, your handsome fiancé is just a fountain of information."

Lowell ejected the cork and poured the champagne into the fluted glasses. He first served his mother, then Grace, Andy and Amy, Henry Curtis, and finally raised his own glass high. "Here's to Andrea Ferguson, the snow maiden I adore, who soon will be my own."

Andy blushed. Lowell always said the right thing. Maybe he'd teach her a thing or two about the social amenities. Grace had certainly tried, but Andy had never been a willing student. Perhaps things would change now. Everything was moving so rapidly her head was spinning, and she knew she was expected to say something next.

"Here's to all of you," she said. She felt totally at a loss. The champagne was fizzy, but her toast was flat.

"Thank you, dear," said Grace. "That was sweet of you." Andy knew she didn't mean it.

"We're really all together to get to know each other and discuss our wedding plans," continued Grace. "But first, Margaret and Henry..."

Andy felt the blood rise in her already flushed face. Somehow she knew Mr. and Mrs. Curtis did not want her mother to call them by their first names.

"Do remember two weeks from Saturday we're having a little engagement party in Newton for Andrea and Lowell. I sent you an invitation. We're mostly having their friends, but naturally you're expected. We'll have a tent, of course, for the young people to dance. It's really going to be a quite simple affair."

A tent, thought Andy. Grace had never said a word about any of this before. She'd just asked Lowell for a list of his friends and Andy'd given her a list of her *Trib* gang. Would she always be doing things to please Grace? No, but this was no time for her to hurt her mother's feelings.

"Thank you, Grace. If Lowell wants us there, we'll be there," said Mrs. Curtis, smiling at her adored son. "But we're here tonight to talk about the wedding plans. Six weeks doesn't give us much time. In fact, it rather takes my breath away. As the bride's mother, you'll be doing the wedding, naturally. We deeply appreciate being included in your thoughts. We'll have the rehearsal dinner, of course. Lowell thinks The Chilton Club is a bit stuffy, so we've engaged The Somerset."

"Who will come to the rehearsal dinner?" asked Andy.

"Oh, just the bridal party and out-of-town guests. And any relatives, of course."

Andy realized that Lowell and she had never discussed a bridal party. There was nobody Andy wanted except Amy. She wondered if Lowell really wanted all those people she'd never met who hung out at The Beachcomber. Oh, no, that just wasn't possible . . . or was it?

A tinkling bell jarred Andy from her thoughts. Mrs. Curtis stood up and in a sonorous voice announced, "Dinner is served." Then Mrs. Curtis smiled at Lowell. It was the only time her face actually lit up. "Lowell, dear, would you escort your old mother to dinner?"

"I'd be charmed, Mother," said Lowell, without a sideward glance at Andy. Henry Curtis took Andy's arm and, followed by Grace and Amy, they all trailed down the winding staircase to the front foyer and then down another half-flight of stairs. To the left Andy saw a small kitchen with Maureen bustling about. To the right, under the living room, Andy supposed, was a large, formal dining room with doors opening onto a brick terrace. A cherrywood sideboard was laden with silver dishes filled with brussel sprouts, new potatoes, and a roast beef. Andy hadn't seen a rib roast since Denver three Christmases ago, when Ben had presided. "I'll have to sell a heap of books to make up for all these ribs," he'd said, his eyes twinkling. It had been his last Christmas.

"Lowell, dear, you'll carve, of course," said Grace, interrupting Andy's musing. Poor Henry, he was always such a bystander.

The table, bathed in candlelight, was covered with a white damask cloth. There were full settings of china and silver, wine- and water glasses, and a bowl stood in the center filled with yellow and white tulips—Andy thought it looked just like a display at Shreve's.

"Everybody, help yourself," said Mrs. Curtis. "We didn't used to have everything passed, but you just can't find good servants these days, so we just rough it a bit."

"Everything looks so pretty," gushed Amy. "Don't you think so, Andrea?"

Andy was watching Lowell adroitly carving the roast. He just never seemed to do anything wrong.

"Now, Andrea, you grab a plate, help yourself, and come sit by Mr. Curtis. Grace, you sit by Andrea; Lowell, you'll sit by me, of course, and Amy on the other side. Henry, will you pour the burgundy? Remember, Lowell. You and I bought this bottle in Beaune. I've been saving it."

"Mother, you're always so thoughtful," said Lowell as he heaped his plate and sat down beside his mother. Andy noticed that Amy seemed spellbound.

"This is exquisite, Margaret," said Grace. "I only wish Ben were here to see."

Andy, who was trying hard not to drip the red wine on the tablecloth, couldn't imagine how even her beloved father would handle such a situation. She knew he'd grin and bear it for his Andy, but she shuddered to think what he'd say to her afterward.

"We're planning to have the wedding at Trinity

THE BEST MAN 119

Church, of course," said Grace. "Andrea, I thought it'd be nice to let Margaret arrange the flowers there since I hear she's been head of the altar guild for so long."

Boy, Mom had certainly covered every angle.

"Well, I'd be pleased, of course," said Mrs. Curtis.

"That's what Mom and I figured," said Amy. "And, as I'm sure you know, we're going to have the reception at The Ritz."

Andy tried to control herself. She felt she was being thwarted, and it wasn't a good feeling at all. *She* should be announcing all this. Not Amy.

Andy glanced at Lowell, who was serenely cutting his rare beef. Why was she so touchy? Why did everything seem all wrong? She had gone over all this with her mother. She had agreed, but suddenly she was all mixed up. The Ritz, 250 guests—why? It seemed so pretentious, not at all the way she wanted to start off her life with Lowell. Was this the way Lowell wanted it? They'd never really discussed the plans thoroughly. Just what had they discussed?

Andy stabbed a new potato and jammed it into her mouth. Grace glared at her. Andy could hear her voice from the past. *Now, Andrea, put little portions on your fork. That's what ladies do.*

Grace took a small sip of the claret wine. "I've already talked to Maurice at The Ritz. He's going to reserve the ballroom for us. All we need from you is a list, maybe sometime in the next two weeks, so we can send the names to the calligrapher. A friend of Amy's knows a wonderful calligrapher. It's a good idea, don't you think so, Margaret?"

"Oh, I do," interrupted Lowell, smiling broadly. "Tami, Sandy, Skip, and Jilly—if he still is with Jilly in June—they'll all think that's a perfect hoot. I guess I'll ask Skip to be my best man."

Andy wondered once again why Roby wasn't mentioned, but they all seemed so flushed with excitement she decided not to rock anybody's yacht.

"What time are you planning the wedding?" asked Mrs. Curtis.

"We thought four-thirty would be appropriate," said Grace, looking under the candelabrum at Andy, who shrugged her shoulders.

"Always have your wedding when the hands of the clock are going up. That's what I heard," said Amy. "Oh, it's all going to be so beautiful. I can hardly wait. I'm just dying to meet all your friends, Lowell. Will they all be at the engagement party?"

"They sure will."

"Andy gave me and Mom *carte blanche* on all engagement-party arrangements. It really ought to be a bash. Mom found a terrific caterer, and I heard of a zingy disco group."

Zingy disco group, thought Andy. Whose engagement party is this? Amy's or mine? Lowell likes disco, too. She remembered how well he danced and almost regretted not taking up her mother's offer of dancing lessons back in high school.

Amy continued, "Mom thought there should just

be background music at the tying of the knot, so I thought *this* party should be fun, fun, fun."

"I know a wicked fish-house punch," said Lowell, winking at Amy.

Swell, thought Andy.

Maureen whisked away the plates, Spode, Andrea noted after her lesson at Shreve's, and returned with a platter of tiny, exhausted peach tarts.

"I didn't have time to have anything made," said Mrs. Curtis. "Ellen Buffington was here all morning about altar guild funding, so I just picked these up at Busken's."

"They don't look so hot, Mother," said Lowell.

"You're absolutely right. Let's retire to the living room for coffee and liqueurs."

"Great idea," said Lowell. "We'll lead the way." He walked around to Andy, pinched her waist, and said, "Come on, beautiful. Enough of this. Up, up, and away."

Andy wished the two of them were indeed going away instead of just back up to the living room. They all seemed to be talking at once, their conversation heightened by the wine.

"Mom said we can get the bridal dresses at Priscilla's," said Amy.

"Thank you for including us in the wedding plans," said Mrs. Curtis. "I guess Henry will have to get out his cutaway."

"Everybody in his best bib and tucker for the big day," laughed Lowell.

The chatter was suddenly interrupted by a flustered, bright-eyed Maureen announcing the arrival of a tall, slender young man with shoulder-length blond hair and high cheekbones. He wore jeans, a blue sweatshirt, and combat boots. So this was Roby, the black sheep. Interesting, thought Andy.

"Well, well. The whole *mishpocha*," he said. "Oh, I'm sorry. Didn't mean to barge in on a party."

"Well, Roby," laughed Lowell. "To what disaster do we owe the unexpected honor of your presence?"

"Well, big brother, the producers of my play at the Charles found me this cheap little room around the corner, but the landlady turned out to be a real nut. I was rehearsing my big love scene this morning. The next thing I know there's this banging on the door and the old lady's yelling for me to take my girl friend and get out."

"What are you saying, lad?" asked Mr. Curtis with a frown.

"There was no one there but me, Dad. I guess my acting was good enough so the landlady thought I had a real woman with me. I ignored her, but when I got back from rehearsal this evening, all my stuff was outside with a note telling me to leave. She doesn't want unmarried couples in her house." Roby laughed delightedly.

"She sounds perfectly dreadful," said Mrs. Curtis.

"No, she's just a little nutty. But that place is now off of Frank's list of cheap digs, and I need to crash here for a night or two until he finds another place. The play opens in ten days and I don't have any time to look."

"Well, really, dear," said his mother, "if only you'd given us some warning ... I suppose Maureen can make up your old room for tonight."

"Now, Margaret," said her husband, "we haven't seen Roby for ages. He can stay as long as he likes."

"Thanks, Dad, but a couple of nights will do. I'm really tired. I've been rehearsing since ten o'clock this morning. But I've got a good part this time and it may move to New York."

Andy asked what the play was about.

"Well, it's called *The Black-eyed Gypsy*. It's about Gypsies in Scotland and the government closing in on them, taking their fingerprints, making the kids go to the local school. The play's about freedom, I guess, what you have to pay for it."

"Sounds great."

"I play one of the guys who won't go along with the changes. I'm also doing the music."

"I'd really love to see it," said Andy. "What about it, Lowell?"

"Well, sure. I'll have to check my schedule." He turned back to conversing with Amy.

Roby looked at Andy more keenly, then spoke to her in a low voice. "Say, I hear the brother got himself engaged. Is that her ladyship over there?" He glanced toward Amy.

"No. As a matter of fact, I'm her ladyship."

"Sorry. You don't look like Lowell's usual type. I mean, you seem kind of down to earth—and smart."

"Thanks. I guess what you mean is I'm not a glamour puss."

"Speaking of glamour, I ran into a girl named Vicky Turner at one of those SoHo openings. She told me Lowell was spoken for, but she didn't seem to take it too seriously. Any man's fair game to her as long as he has looks and money. She was giving me the eye until I told her that I lived in a railroad walk-up in the East Village with a lady roommate. . . . So, you're my future sister-in-law. I really hope that you can catch the play," he said in a serious tone, then reached into a back pocket. "Here're two tickets for opening night—they're my comps."

"Thanks, Roby. I'll be there. Promise."

While this somewhat muted exchange was going on, coffee and liqueurs were served, and the conversation became more animated. Andy noticed Mrs. Curtis pouring herself another generous helping of cognac, while Mr. Curtis discussed his beloved orchids with Grace, who seemed genuinely fascinated. Amy and Lowell were laughing about something. Suddenly Roby's voice cut through the peaceful chatter.

"Go easy, Mums. You know Doc Sturgis said too much of the sauce is bad for you."

Andy felt that he meant well, but his approach came off as less than tactful.

Mrs. Curtis put down her glass with a shaking hand, then she spoke in a shrill voice. "Robert Curtis! How dare you? First you come barging in here without notice and interrupt a family party dressed like a truck driver, and then you publicly criticize your mother. You've never forgiven me for trying to help you with that Mooney girl."

Roby's eyes turned cold as blue ice.

"I was in love with Sarah Mooney, and I would have married her. But you, dear Mother, had to call her parents and remind them of your high position. Did you threaten to have her father fired from Hopkins-Tyson? Did you? All I know is she left town suddenly, and when I found out about it, she'd disappeared. I hear she's married to some mechanic in south Boston."

"Cut it out, Roby," Lowell intervened. "I saw Sarah last year, and she asked about you. You wouldn't recognize her. She's got three kids, and she's happy. So forget it. It's over. Maybe you'd better stay at my place tonight. Here's the keys."

"Thanks," said Roby with a sigh. "Sorry to have ruined your party. Nice to have met you all." He turned to Andy, looking straight in her eyes. So like Lowell, she thought, and so different. "Hope you enjoy the play. Come backstage and tell me what you think."

"I will," she said.

His exit produced a moment of quiet, followed by an explosion of chatter on every subject but the vanished intruder. Mrs. Curtis sat alone and subdued. Poor woman, Andy thought. She's estranged from her youngest son, all no doubt due because of the best intentions. No wonder she drinks a little too much. The Curtis clan began to appear more vulnerable, and Andy liked them better for it. Grace and Henry had discovered a real horticultural bond, and Amy and Lowell were delighting in exchanging disco stories. She ventured over to sit next to Mrs. Curtis, who gave her a little wry grimace.

"It takes Roby to upset me every time he appears. He was always such a delicate, quiet little boy, so different from Lowell, but now he's completely changed. I'm so sorry. That all wasn't very pleasant."

"Forgive me if I'm talking out of turn," said Andy, "but I got the feeling he really cares about you. He's just too stubborn to say so. Maybe if you could see him alone and really talk it out. . . . "

"You know, Andrea," said Mrs. Curtis, "I was rather surprised when Lowell first sprung you on us. You seemed so different, your background and interests. But perhaps that's not such a bad thing. Thank you for saying what you did. Most people would simply have ignored the whole scene. I'm afraid we have a distaste for family drama, especially played in public."

"Don't worry, Mrs. Curtis. We Fergusons aren't gossips. That's what I hated most when I worked in Denver, reporting the latest chitchat about so-and-so's divorce or paternity suit. I didn't think it was anyone's business, and I still don't."

"Thank you, my dear Andrea. Now if you will excuse me. . ." Mrs. Curtis bade good night to everyone and made her exit with considerable dignity. The Ferguson ladies all rose to thank Mr. Curtis for a delightful evening while he, in turn, urged them to stay.

He was not successful, but Grace promised to call Mrs. Curtis the following day to firm up the wedding agenda. Amy and Lowell were to decide on the music for the engagement shindig.

On the way home, Lowell apologized for Roby's behavior.

"Lowell, it's all right. I can see why he's such a trial for your mother, but I like him. I'm looking forward to the play."

"Hmmm. I just hope it's not full of profanity and nudity like some of his East Village extravaganzas."

"Oh, I doubt it. That's pretty passé these days. Anyway, it's too cold in Scotland for bare buttocks, unless, of course, they're covered by a kilt."

"Andrea, you're outrageous. But I'm glad you two got along."

"Why shouldn't I? As you said, he looks like you, only skinnier."

"Well. I hope you never catch me in combat boots. He might at least have changed."

"Where, Lowell? He didn't have a place to change."

"He could have put on a shirt and jacket, but that's our Roby."

He kissed her and said he'd call the next day. She waved after him, thinking how different two brothers could be. Poor Roby. He was certainly a jarring color in the Curtis family portrait. She breathed a happy sigh of relief—the "summit meeting" was over. Her mother and Amy must be savoring their triumph. Arrangements for both the party and wedding seemed well in hand; their hands. Maybe it was as well. It would leave her more time for her assignment with Tom Bradford.

SEVEN

"HONESTLY, LOWELL, I'M sorry about our date tonight, but it can't be helped. When I mentioned to Pete that the candidate planned to spend the weekend in Truro, he got this nutty idea of sending me up to corner him on his own turf. I'm booked into the Winthrop House. It's an inn or something. Oops!" While attempting to mix tuna and mayonnaise for her lunch bag, the phone Andy was holding precariously between ear and shoulder dropped with a small crash. "Sorry, love. What did you say? Sunday's good, I guess. I think I can get all I need Saturday. Sure. Tennis at four and dinner. Great! Yes, love you, too, darling. 'Bye."

Andy checked her rushed packing: camera, paperback, sleep mask. She added a forgotten toothbrush, and that was it. She hauled her small case down to the VW before starting for work. This way she could write her notes, eat lunch at the paper, and head right down to the Cape at five o'clock. Rush hour was the worst, but maybe it wouldn't be so bad since it was only early May.

At five-fifteen she was piloting her VW through the thick of traffic onto the Mass Turnpike and Route 23. An accident slowed everything down for about twenty minutes. Pete had said she should get there about seven, but that seemed doubtful now. She turned on the radio and learned to her dismay that a thunderstorm was expected in early evening. That was all she needed. Nothing worse than driving in heavy rain. She managed simultaneously to pull out her seat belt and maneuver into a faster lane. When she neared Plymouth, the traffic thinned noticeably.

Her spirits rose. This should be fun. She couldn't wait to see Windswept—her mind conjured a vision of a high white house standing among elms—no, pines maybe—no, just sunlight near the sea. She began to hum an old favorite tune of her father about going to Montana when a big raindrop hit the windshield.

Five minutes later the storm was in full spate. She hoped the brakes would hold. Darn. She knew she should have had the VW checked last weekend, but she'd had to meet Lowell at the club. Priorities, girl. A few miles later she noticed steam coming out of the hood, or was it rain hitting the warm metal? By the time she left Eastham, she was certain it was steam. With sixteen miles to go until Truro, the car started to slow down. "Oh, no," she whispered. "Come on, baby. You can do it. Come on. You're a good little car. Come!" But urgings and flattery proved useless. Two minutes later, she pulled the dying VW onto the shoulder. "Damn, damn, damn!" she raged. She'd have to call someone, but who and where? The only number she had in this area was Tom Bradford's.

She stepped out into the rain, lamenting the ruin of her light tweed jacket and pumps. There hadn't been anything behind her for a couple of miles. Maybe up ahead. She trudged along for about a half a mile until a ghostly light revealed a filling station on her left. Swallowing her dampened pride, she dialed Tom's number. Two, three rings. Finally a voice answered, "Yes, Tom Bradford here."

"Oh, Tom, thank God. It's Andy. My car broke down and I—"

"Where are you?"

"Well, I think I'm in Wellfleet. I'm at a Texaco station. The car's about a half mile back."

"And you walked in this rain? Hang on. I'll be there in less than ten minutes."

She waited, shivering, in the small, chilly office. A short, redheaded man shook his head in sympathy and offered her a Coke. "No—no, thanks," she managed, and smiled wanly. A few minutes later a Jeep pulled up, and out jumped Tom Bradford.

"Hey, Andy. Meet Jim Horton, best mechanic on the Cape. He'll pick up your car tomorrow. Come on, you look done in. We'll go back, get your suitcase, and see about drying you out."

They found the abandoned VW and loaded her things into Tom's Jeep. Then Tom lifted the hood and examined various mysterious hoses and valves.

"Looks like a busted hose," he called. "Don't worry. Jim can fix anything."

Tom carefully drove the remaining distance to Truro and up the winding driveway to Windswept. Andy caught a hazy glimpse of white porch and glowing windows.

"Welcome to Windswept," he said, guiding her into the warm kitchen. "Take off those wet things, and I'll run you a tub in a jiffy."

Andy struggled out of her sodden jacket while Tom poured a garnet-colored liquid into a glass.

"This should warm you up."

"Um—good," she said as she drank it down. "What is it?"

"Beach-plum brandy. Fill a jar with beach plums, throw in some sugar and as much vodka as you have around, wait six months, and presto! Not the real thing, but it's all I've got in that line. Come on, get out of those clothes while I start your bath."

Too tired to protest, she followed him up the wide stairway. An almost forgotten childhood feeling came over her—the warm embrace of an old, cherished house. He indicated a room on the right.

"You can sleep there tonight if you like. Here,

let me plug in the heater. There's a fireplace, but that'll take too long."

Andy closed the door and stared at the huge brass bed, covered by a tufted spread, with a heavy quilt folded at its foot. The room looked warm and cozy, but God, she was *still* freezing. She stepped into the large, white bathroom, already clouded with steam, then quickly undressed and slid into the old-fashioned iron tub. Were those claws underneath? It felt wonderful. Even the soap smelled familiar, bringing back memories of her first home. She was almost dozing in comfort and nostalgia when it suddenly occurred to her that she hadn't called the Winthrop House.

Reluctantly she pulled herself out of the steamy bath and dashed for the bedroom, now pleasantly warmed by the heater. She pawed through her suitcase for her jeans. Oh, no! She could see them flung on the bedside chair at Linneaen Street where they no doubt still rested. Oh, well. She pulled on her black silk jersey trousers and jade green cashmere sweater. Too posh, she thought, but not to be helped.

"Wow," said Tom as she entered the kitchen. "I didn't know I was entertaining a glamour girl for dinner."

"Don't get me wrong," she said, "I seem to have left my jeans at home, by mistake. Now look. You've done more than enough. Let me just call the Winthrop House and tell them I'm alive and hungry." "Let's see," he said, glancing at the big kitchen clock.

"Dinner went off about ten minutes ago. All

you'll get is a sandwich. Now, what we have here is Portuguese soup, homemade brown bread, and while you were remaking yourself, I located a bottle of Scotch. Go on, call them, Andy—I'll get the number—and tell them you'll see them tomorrow. The big bedroom is yours for the night."

"Well, okay. If it's really no bother."

"None at all, and it'll save us time in the morning if you expect to go clamming with me. That should make good copy. 'How the candidate unwinds.' The weather report swears it'll be fine by seven A.M."

She smiled happily. "I'd love it. That bed looks so comfortable, I had to resist leaping into it the moment I saw it."

Tom heated the soup, which was thick and spicy with Portuguese and Spanish sausages, kale, and kidney beans. Andy had two bowls and a thick slice of bread.

"Tom, I could eat that stuff forever, especially that homemade bread. It's fantastic."

"Well, I'll tell you a little secret. My neighbor, Mrs. Souza, makes it for me. A few years ago, I did her a legal favor. Nothing really, but I knew she couldn't afford it so I charged her a dozen loaves of brown bread, and she's been supplying me ever since. If she keeps it up, she'll have overpaid me at least twice."

"Now, that's the kind of story we want," said Andy with enthusiasm. "The readers will love it. You can use the bread part if you like but not the favor. There's a lot of pride in these parts. Manny Souza used to run his own fishing boat out of Provincetown. Then the fishing got thin in the fifties and sixties—lots of dredgers and big commercial boats horning in. It finally didn't pay, so he retired and moved down here near his folks. Now he carves little boats and animals for one of the gift shops. Annie helps out with her bread. She supplies one of the fancy food shops in Wellfleet. Now, let's light the fire in the parlor and have some of that Scotch."

Andy watched Tom roll sheets of newspaper and carefully crisscross the kindling on top. Finally he built a low tepee with the logs.

"That's funny," she said. "My dad always made a fire just like that. He learned that from an Indian . . . said they did it that way to make it draw better."

"What's funnier," said Tom, "is that I learned this from a Norwegian, and he said the same thing."

"You know, there's something about this place—the fire and all—that reminds me of our old ranch in Colorado."

"Well, that's a new side. You're full of sides, aren't you? More secrets than a pirate's chest. I thought of taking you sailing tomorrow if the wind is right, but maybe you'd rather ride instead. We used to keep horses here, but my folks got too old, and I got too ambitious, so we sold them to the neighbors up the road. A friend of mine, Boyzeen Simmons, has a stable back in Provincetown. I'm sure he'd give us a couple of nags tomorrow."

"Oh, Tom, I'd love it. I haven't ridden in years. No time and too expensive in Boston."

"Go on, tell me all about the ranch."

"Hey, who's interviewing whom?"

"Well, you weren't scheduled to see me until tomorrow, so this is all free time." Andy was always a little hesitant to mention her father in conversation. His sudden death had left an emptiness in her heart that not even Lowell could seem to fill.

"Well, let's see. I had this horse called Mexico. I loved that animal. One summer one of Mom's fancy Boston cousins, Jim Littleton, came out to see 'the real West.' You should have seen his face when he realized there wasn't a telephone, no electricity, just gas lamps. He asked us what we did in the evenings, and Dad put on his best twang. 'Well, sometimes we light a fire, tell stories, and sing cowboy songs. Sometimes we set and look up at the stars. Most times we just mosey up to bed.'"

"Go on. I love your Western imitation."

"Imitation nothing. That's just the real me exaggerated a little."

"So exaggerate some more."

"Well, Uncle Littleton told a lot of snooty stories about riding to the hounds in Pennsylvania and Ireland. Then he said he wouldn't mind trying a Western horse if it had real spirit. Dad warned him about Mexico and his little tricks, but he wouldn't listen. Hadn't he ridden over the worst bogs and hedges in Ireland?

"Off he went the next morning, stiff boots and all. As soon as Mexico spotted his favorite tree, he took off under a low branch like a Derby winner. Poor Uncle Littleton got knocked into the mud. I felt kind of sorry for him until he told Dad 'the damned brute should be put down.' Anyway, I secretly gave Mexico an apple and took off with him by myself. I loved that horse."

Tom poured two small Scotches. He handed one to Andy and poked up the fire. She smelled the pine resin.

"Drink that, Andy, my little cowgirl. Pretty soon you'll be dreaming sweet dreams about Mexico and leading a stampede of horses to the polls to elect the future congressman, Tom Bradford."

"You know, Tom," she said, smiling drowsily, "I really think you have a good chance. That speech at Barnstable was wonderful."

"Did you hear it?"

"Yes, I caught some of it on the late news—I love your haircut, by the way—and I could see the crowd was really moved by your words. People aren't as dumb as Sorley thinks they are. They want to hear the bread-and-butter issues, not just corny jokes and 'I love you all' stuff."

Tom laughed. "Wait till I tell you what I pulled last Sunday." He launched into a rather complicated anecdote involving Sorley and the licensing commission. He glanced at Andy. She was smiling faintly, but her eyes were shut, her breathing soft and even. He stifled a desire to kiss her eyes, her mouth. Instead, he sighed, lifted her gently in his arms, and carried her up to the large bedroom. Andy was half-awake but too pleasurably embarrassed to say anything until they reached the door.

"It's okay, Tom. I can manage. Really."

He released her gently. Damn it, he thought, she

felt so good, smelled so good. But he only said, "Good night, then. I'll be back around six-thirty."

"Good night, Tom. Thanks for everything."

Andy slipped into her flannel nightgown and snuggled into the soft, comfortable bed. The wind still howled and rain beat on the window, but she was far away, riding Mexico through fields of columbine on the high mesa....

Curled in the big brass bed, Andy's dreams changed during the night. She was sliding from a horse. But now it seemed to be happening on the Boston Common and a tall dark-haired man was pulling her to her feet. "You should be okay," the stranger was saying, "knock on wood." *Knock, knock, knock.* She woke to a real knocking at her door.

"Six-thirty, Andy. Better hurry if we're going to catch the tide."

What tide? She opened her eyes to the large, cozy room and saw the first golden rays of sun sliding over the windowsill. He was right! You could see the ocean.

"I'll be right there, Tom."

As his quick footsteps receded down the stairs, she remembered the forgotten jeans and raced to the door.

"Tom, have you got some old jeans I could borrow?"

"Sure thing. I'd better get you a shirt, too." A few minutes later he produced both. "You won't need shoes when we get there," he said. "Do you mind going barefoot?"

"I never used to wear shoes from June to September. One summer my feet were so tough you could light matches on my heels."

"Well, come on, then. Coffee's ready."

Andy jammed herself into the pants, which fit pretty well except around the waist. Thank God for long legs. The red-and-black-checked woolen shirt enveloped her. Well, nobody's taking my picture, she thought. There was bread and coffee on the table.

"Hurry up," he said. "We'll have breakfast afterward."

She grabbed her camera, a big hunk of Mrs. Souza's bread, and jumped into the Jeep.

"Here's the thing," he said. "The lowest ebb tide is once a month, at the full moon. That's when you get sea clams. May, June, and July are the best months. Later on they're hard to find. The law says one bucket per person. Since you're writing this up and maybe taking a picture, it wouldn't do for a conservationist candidate to get more."

"You're right," she laughed. "It could blow the whole campaign. Andy Ferguson never lies!"

They made a turn or two, then followed the road to its end.

"Here," he said as they jumped down from the Jeep, "I'll take the rakes. Can you handle the bucket?"

Barefoot, they scrambled down the dune to where the sand stretched out, clear and unmarked before them. "Now we head for the buoy out there just to the right and start looking for air holes."

Sure enough, she began to see small holes. "Here, Tom. Over here!"

"Take this rake," he said, "and dig."

Andy pushed the rake vigorously into the sand and was rewarded with a large clam. "Wow! I used to have one of these as an ashtray."

"But I bet you never tasted the inside. That's the real treat." Tom bent to his task with enthusiasm. The sun had risen over the dune and shone down warmly on the flats and sparkling water.

"Wait—keep digging while I take a shot," Andy said. She grabbed for the camera around her neck, adjusted the light meter, focused, then snapped. His neck, so recently shorn on her orders, looked suddenly vulnerable. Yes, he looked right in his jeans and blue workshirt. The bucket was half-full now. She raked out another half-dozen clams, then dashed out into the incoming tide for a long shot.

"Hey! Careful, there. I've dried you out once already." He glanced up, smiling, his shock of dark hair grazing his forehead, his face ruddy with exertion.

"That's terrific," she shouted, and clicked.

"Well, the bucket's full," he said, "and I told you that's all we're allowed to take. Come on. I'm hungry. We'll stop at Dutra's for some provisions."

While he shopped, Andy wrote up her clamming notes in a shorthand only she could decipher. Then Tom revved up the Jeep, and they drove back to Windswept in the glimmering morning sunlight. He stowed the gear and lugged the bucket into the kitchen. Silently he took two tumblers from a cabinet, picked up a curved knife, and slit the tough muscle on four clams. He poured the liquid from the clams into the glasses. After this, he produced tomato juice and a bottle of vodka from the brown shopping bag. He measured carefully and then poured the mixture over the clam juice. Whistling, he stirred the concoction and handed one to Andy.

"Old Bradford tradition," he said. "Here's to you, pretty Andy. You're the first girl I've ever taken clamming. I used to think they'd cramp my style, but you're different. You've got your own style. I like it."

They drank their bloody marys, and she cooked ham and eggs while he handled toast and fresh coffee.

"Um, that must be the biggest breakfast I've eaten for years." She smiled and stretched comfortably. "But we have work to do. I've got to get this copy in by Monday so it can hit the Wednesday special section."

"Fine with me," he said. "Where do we start?"

"Right here with some of the local people you know, the ones you deal with."

"By the way, speaking of them," said Tom, "I'd better get Horton on the blower right now. If you're lucky, he can fix your car and have it ready before five."

"Gosh, that would be great," she said.

"He's a good friend, and there's not much business yet. You're lucky this wasn't Memorial Day weekend. Anyway, I've got plans for us after that."

Andy subdued her curiosity and decided to wait for the surprise.

That morning they visited the Souzas. Andy praised Mrs. Souza's bread and took their pictures. Next, they drove to the big wharf in Wellfleet to interview some fishermen, then to Al Tasha, the real estate broker. Andy took notes as Tom and Al discussed the real estate crisis. Al asked if Gene Sorley had any chance of getting a bill through the House to eliminate several miles of the national seashore.

"Not a chance," said Tom. "Kennedy made that pretty foolproof. The people around here wouldn't stand for it."

"They might not, but it's the big real estate people who have the lobby money."

Andy wrote furiously in her big notebook. At three they returned to Windswept. It now looked much as she had pictured it—a little shabby in places, needing paint, but fine and stately in its grove of locust trees. The grass underneath them was already green and some brave daffodils glowed yellow as the sunlight.

"It's beautiful," she said. "How come it's so green here and not down the hill?"

"It's the trees," he said. "Locusts put lots of nitrogen in the soil—that's what daffs need. It's cooperation. What we need more of in government."

They sat lazily sipping coffee when Tom asked her how she had gotten into journalism. She told him about her father's press in Denver, how he had encouraged her from the beginning to write stories about real events. "Like how our pet rabbit, Samantha, had her babies in our living room or when I helped put out our neighbor's fire. He told me always to report exactly what I saw and never to get personally involved."

"That's fine," said Tom, "but when you get beyond simply reporting—say, if you have your own column—you have to have a point of view. You know, after that first interview, I asked Chip to get me some of your old pieces. You can be terrific when you get indignant, like the one about the shelters, and that other one about the crooked Cambridge councilman. I wouldn't want you against me. You're a fine newsperson, Ferguson. Stick to it."

"I intend to."

The ringing of the phone interrupted them. It was Jim Horton calling to announce his success with the car.

"Only the water hose. Didn't have to send for any parts."

"Good man, Jim. We'll be right over."

Andy gratefully paid, patted the hood of her VW, and followed Tom back home.

"Now, Bradford," she said, "what's the big surprise?"

"We're going for a ride."

They drove the ten miles to Provincetown and as they dipped down the hill toward High Head, the whole glittering bay spread itself out beneath them.

"You know," he said, "this is the seventh greatest natural harbor in the world."

"No kidding. What are the others?"

"Oh, you know. Singapore, Hong Kong—"

"Hey, look at those dunes!" The great sand hills rose, wind-sculpted and pure with little tufts of sword grass and beach roses in hollows. "I'd love to walk them sometime."

They continued as far as the last sign into town, turned right toward the salt marsh, and halted in front of a white fence facing a stable.

"Oh, Tom, is this your friend's place? Boyzeen Simmons, was that his name?"

"What a memory. No wonder you're good. He said he'd have two fresh horses ready at five."

Andy's eyes glowed as the horses were led out. A trim chestnut named Bobby was hers and a somewhat larger roan, Mashpee, went to Tom.

"I'm not really used to Eastern saddles," she said as Tom let the stirrups down for her long legs, "but I'll manage."

They started off through a long meadow that led into a narrow path in the woods. "We'll just take it easy for a while until they get used to us," said Tom. "Of course, Mashpee's an old friend, aren't you, buddy?" Tom patted Mashpee's neck.

"I can tell he likes you. Where did he get that name?"

"The Mashpees were the last of the local Indians. There's a town with that name down the Cape. Come on. We can try a little canter now." Tom touched Mashpee's flank gently with his heel. "Watch the branches, they won't knock you off, but you may want to duck a little."

Breathless, they emerged on top of a low dune facing the Atlantic.

"What's over there?" gasped Andy.

"Oh, Portugal, the blue Azores."

They guided their horses to the beach and watched in silence as the colors of sunset streaked the sky with gold, rose, and purple.

"Look," he said. "You can see the moon rising. Isn't that great? By the time we get back it should be full up."

Slowly they let the horses splash through the small shore waves.

"Better head home now," said Tom. "There's a trail near here that runs into the first one."

"If you say so," Andy agreed reluctantly.

By the time they reached the meadow, the full moon shone high and bright. Andy could see Tom's high cheekbones and strong features clearly. Suddenly, the horses scented home and, without warning, they started to gallop full out to the stable.

"You all right?" he yelled.

"Fine," she shouted, clutching Bobby's sides.

Then all caution fled. They hooted, laughed, and hung on until the panting horses and riders reached the stable yard. Andy's legs were shaking, not visibly, she hoped. Her cheeks were rosy with exertion and excitement.

"Gosh, Tom," she said, climbing into the Jeep, "I haven't had so much fun since the Jordan boys took me riding in Steamboat Springs. I tore my shirt half off on a barbed-wire fence galloping just like that. We felt so good we decided to get a drink at the Palace Hotel. Torn shirt and all, I sauntered in with them like we were the Dalton Gang. Billy played the one-armed bandit and won the jackpot. One hundred silver dollars. We stayed for dinner and wine. The boys had cigars."

"How old were you, tomboy?" he asked while maneuvering the Jeep down the dark road.

"Eighteen. Underage, of course, but I was always tall. The next day we got a terrible bawling out when our parents heard. We had to say we were sorry, but we weren't. That was wonderful, and so was this. I wasn't sure I was going to stay on! But I did . . . Do you come here often?"

"Not really. I haven't had time and in a few weeks there'll be too many tourists around. But I agree—that's the best ride I've had in years."

In mutual contentment, they drove back in the moonlight.

"What are those bushes over there?" she asked as they neared the driveway.

"That's beach plum. In another week or so, when they're in full bloom, you'll think it's been snowing here. Maybe you'll see them?" The question sounded in his voice.

"That would be nice," she murmured. "Now what?"

"Sea-clam pie, of course. I mix up the clams with my secret ingredients known only to Bradford men, throw them in a crust, pop it in the oven while we have a drink, and *voilà*, dinner for two, chez Windswept."

"That's much nicer than chez anything else," said Andy without thinking. Suddenly, she remembered Chez Bernice and Stowe, and she felt uncomfortable.

"Okay, pardner, grub will be ready in fifteen minutes. Would you like a Cape Codder or is that too corny for your paper?"

"It probably is, but I'll have one anyway. Vodka and cranberry juice, right?"

After dinner, Andy walked around the hall and parlor, admiring the paintings—a mixture of old whaling canvases and simple contemporary watercolors. "Where did you find these?" she asked.

"The newer ones are mostly by artists who live here, some year round."

"I really love this one," she said, staring at a small seascape signed *Resika*.

"Oh, that's one of Paul's. It's an old warehouse at the end of the wharf. They're having a town meeting next week to decide whether to tear it down or make it into cheap rooms for the kids who work here in the summer. There's even one group of folks who want to turn it into a theater."

"What do you want? Don't tell me. Cheap rent for waiters."

"Yes, and a small theater as well. Plenty of parking room." Tom built a fire and lit a candle. They could see the moonlight through the trees.

"We used to cook outside on a big wagon wheel over a pit," Andy told him. "After supper, Dad would put on more wood. We'd watch the stars and swap stories. He knew a lot of old Western stuff and poems like 'The Face on the Barroom Floor.' Even Mom and Amy liked those times, though I know they weren't as keen on the ranch as we were."

"You really miss your dad," said Tom. "He sounds like a terrific guy."

Without warning, tears flooded her eyes. "Oh, God, I'm sorry . . . but sometimes I miss him so much it hurts."

Tom gently put his arm around her and stroked her hair. He kissed her cheek, then her nose and eyes. "It's all right, Andy," he whispered. "I'll be your friend if you'll let me. You're the loveliest woman I've ever known. I mean it. This place even likes you. It doesn't feel empty now." Then suddenly he was kissing her mouth.

"Tom—please, Tom," she managed. "I can't. There's something I haven't told you. It's . . ." Why weren't the words coming?

"Don't, sweetheart. Don't talk," he whispered, smoothing her curls.

Andy straightened up with a jolt. "Please, Tom. I have to go now. This has been the nicest day I can think of, but I must leave. Now!" Her bag, already packed, stood next to the stairway, and she went swiftly to it. "Don't show me out. I know the way."

"Good-bye, Ms. Ferguson," he said coldly. "Maybe I'll see you next week. Wrap things up." His eyes, so warm only a moment before, now looked black and impenetrable as onyx.

"Oh, for God's sake, Tom, don't be angry. I'm just terribly confused. I'll call you. 'Bye."

* * *

The short drive to the Winthrop House was a medley of conflicting thoughts. Why didn't she just say she was engaged to Lowell? Why? He'd probably think Lowell was some kind of playboy. Well, isn't he? she questioned herself. No, he's my future husband. He's fun and sweet—and rich.

I hope I haven't made an awful mistake, thought Andy. I think I love Lowell. But Tom—he's so different, so real.

Stop it, Andy. You've made your bed. Now lie in it . . . Her mind recalled the vision of the large brass bed in the upstairs bedroom—No! Stop this! she told herself.

Andy pulled the VW over onto the grass, combed her unruly curls, applied fresh lipstick, and arrived at the inn with a modicum of self-possession.

"We've been expecting you, Miss Ferguson," said the lady at the desk. "Lowell Curtis called last night. Said he was your fiancé. My, aren't you lucky. He sounded worried to death, but I assured him you were in good hands." She smiled ingratiatingly.

Andy thanked her, forced a smile back, and climbed to a small, charming room with a crocheted spread and samplers on the wall. She knew she ought to phone Lowell now. The last two days seemed to have pulled her back to a pre-Lowell time in her life. Most of all, it was the lovely old house, Windswept, with its woody smells mixed with plain soap and furniture polish. Even the prints and quilts and the old-fashioned range seemed like dear friends from childhood. In Col-

THE BEST MAN

orado, their house was newer and smaller, and the trees had been pines and aspens, but the same feeling was there—something solid, safe, and welcoming. Then, oh God, there was that ride. She had gone back in time eight years. Lowell seemed strangely distant, part of another glamorous life—a life she had been playing at, but had never truly entered with her soul.

And there was Tom Bradford. She knew how much he liked her. Oh, why kid herself? He was lonely, involved in his work. She had landed on his doorstep practically gift-wrapped. No wonder he had fallen for her. This scenario was reminding her of herself and Lowell. Lonely workaholic spinster meets golden boy—cut it out!

"That's not why Tom likes me. . . . He thinks I'm a good sport," she told herself as she began to prepare for bed. "Well, I am. He likes my looks, which is okay. But he really seems to like my mind. Likes the way I think and write."

She really believed Tom when he said he had read her old stuff and liked it. That was odd. Lowell and she never talked much about her work. Sometimes she thought he was jealous. Maybe it was because he wanted her all to himself. But was it Andy he wanted or that Andrea lady who was smart, sassy, Western cute, and so different from the contessas and rich girls he'd known? she wondered. . . .

Andy knew Lowell was fun and handsome, but she had to admit that the money scared her a little, all those dinner parties and dances. Maybe she was just a little scared of the commitment. Wasn't that it? Tom seemed more ordinary, she guessed, more down home, so naturally she felt comfortable with him. She felt more like her old self. Her true self?

Lowell made her feel different, more exciting, but sometimes she felt like she was in a movie and he was directing it. Come to think of it, he seemed to make all the decisions for both of them. In a way it was nice, full of surprises, like always being on a high. Only sometimes she felt like she was missing something important. . . .

"I should be floating in bliss," she said aloud to the bright moon as she snapped off the light and climbed into bed. "Two wonderful guys crazy about me. They both cook better than I do. They're both great looking. Lowell's handsomer, of course. Oh, God, it's so confusing. If I'm so darn lucky and in such good hands, why do I feel so rotten?"

The moon had no answers for her as she drifted off to sleep, vaguely aware that she had failed to call Lowell. . . .

EIGHT

SUNDAY WAS ANOTHER perfect day. She drove up the Cape trying not to look to the left as she passed the turn for Windswept. She wondered how Tom had slept, how she had allowed things to go so far without clueing him in on Lowell. Of course, it was part of her training. "Never get too personal with your subject." But hadn't everything been personal from the moment she had called him for help? Something about Windswept had made her vulnerable. Yet she had tried to keep everything professional until Tom made it impossible. Of course, it wasn't his fault. For all he knew, she was as unattached as he, and they had been close together for more than twenty-four hours.

She arrived at her apartment about noon, unpacked, and spread her notes on the kitchen table. She could complete her profile tonight and have the finished copy and films all set for Monday morning. Pete would be pleased.

She was ready when Lowell rapped. For some reason the familiar knock seemed silly and rather juvenile. When she answered, he stared at her questioningly.

"What happened? Why didn't you call? And where the hell did you spend Friday night? I was worried you got caught in that storm, and then when I called the inn at ten and you weren't there, I figured that car of yours might have conked out."

"I'll tell you the whole ghastly saga at dinner. If we don't leave now, we won't get our court."

Lowell played with more than his usual intensity, slamming overheads and slashing volleys across the net. They said little. After beating her soundly, he smiled an apology.

"Sorry for playing rough. It's just that I missed you this weekend, and I don't know ... there's something different about you. What happened with your candidate guy? Is he trying to horn in on my territory?"

"What an expression. No, I don't think he has any territorial plans. Naturally, I didn't talk about us. Not professional. My car broke down, one of the pipes or something; I called Bradford for help, and he let me stay in his huge house for the night. It seemed sensible since I wanted to do a piece on the candidate clamming, and they have to do that at sunrise, at low tide."

"Oh, I see. Then I suppose you spent the whole day with the guy? Did he take you out for a cozy New England dinner, ply you with aphrodisiacs, and make a pass?"

"Don't be silly, Lowell. Look, I'll go home, change, and I'll see you at six."

"Where do you feel like going?"

"Oh, I don't care, somewhere simple, not too dressy."

"Let's try The Beachcomber. I've been threatening to take you there for ages."

"Fine. See you then."

At half past six they pulled off Route 128, north of Boston, and drove toward the water until a small pink neon sign announced their destination. The outside was plain, almost austere, but within a great deal had been spent on chrome fixtures, black-and-pink Art Deco wallpaper, and black marble-topped tables with tubular black and chrome chairs. On each table were lamps of svelte black ladies holding up pink parasols and bud vases, each with a perfect rose.

"Isn't it great?" said Lowell. "They can only take about thirty a night for dinner, reservations at least a week in advance. It's run by Skip Sturgis, my ex-roomie from Harvard. Remember, I told you he dropped out of Sullivan and Pierce when he'd made almost enough to open this place. Some of us made small investments, so we're all pulling for his success. There's a lot of the old crowd around as a rule." A lilting voice from the bar saluted them.

"Lowell honey, long time no see."

"Oh, Jilly. Great to see you. I'd like you to meet my fiancée, Andrea Ferguson."

Andy smiled and shook hands with a redheaded girl, appropriately clad in a silver-and-black pant suit with a pink chiffon scarf. "I'll tell Skip you're here. He's having some problem with a shrimp delivery. Not fresh enough! Well, he should talk . . ." She slid a little unsteadily off her stool and swayed her way toward a back room.

"Is she a regular or something?" Andy asked.

"She's Skip's current lady. They don't usually last very long, I'm afraid. He prefers them a little dumb and then, eventually, they bore him. But he says he can't seem to get attracted to girls he can talk to."

"Boy! He's in trouble."

"Not really. His real love is this place. If it's going well, he's happy. What do you say to frozen margaritas? They're terrific here."

"Sounds good, but just regular for me, with salt. The frozen ones go straight to my forehead like a hammer."

"You're supposed to sip, not gulp, and how did you get to be such an expert?"

"Lowell, Denver was into margaritas long before Boston. Not everything started here. I'm really not an expert but I do like them."

Lowell ordered and they scarcely had time for a sip when the door swung open and a noisy group headed in their direction.

"Hey, Lowell. What's new? How are the Bedouin girls? Or were they French this time? Oh, uh, sorry."

Lowell introduced Andy to Somebody Benson, Sandy Someone, Vicky, and the young man who had greeted them, Ivor Smith. Sandy looked as perky as her name, and Vicky was a real beauty, raven haired and pale with a large, sensuous mouth and perfect teeth. She seated herself on Lowell's other side and began whispering to him. Lowell, to Andy's chagrin, whispered back.

Finally Skip arrived, full of bonhomie. He flung his arm around Lowell's back, kissed Vicky and Sandy, and bowed to Andy on being introduced. "Hey, glad to see you guys. The whole cast of *The House That Jack Built* is coming after the show. They're opening in New York next week, so stick around. Michael Morkin is a howl as long as he keeps his clothes on. He says margaritas always bring out his barbarian side."

"Sounds like they bring out more than his side," giggled Sandy. "Say, Skipper, how about some goodies? We'll take the big table. Marny and Joe may be in later."

Andy found herself shuffled to a long table in back with Lowell at the head and Vicky sitting opposite her. While bowls of guacamole, refried beans, nachos, and salsas appeared and more drinks were ordered, she wondered if this would be her crowd in the years to come. How would the guys at the paper fit in with their wise-acre cracks and rumpled sports jackets?

These people were all attractive and casual chic. Everyone seemed to be talking at once. Commodities, someone's party that conflicted with the Symphony benefit, condos. Had they heard that

Tracy Byrd had opened a reggae disco, but three of the musicians got busted for possession the second night? Did you hear the one about Princess Anne and her horse? Lowell and Vicky seemed to be having a private tête-à-tête, while on her right, Ivor was trying on Sandy's little black hat. Skip pulled up a stool between Lowell and herself and after asking her what she thought of the place, wondered if she couldn't write something about it in "Painting the Town."

"Well, restaurants aren't really my beat. That's more Jen Fox's territory. But I'll get her to come out if she already hasn't. I'm more into City Hall and public officials. But didn't The Beachcomber get a big play in *Boston Magazine* last fall? That's right. They loved the Art Deco and Mexican specialties."

"What a memory. But they were here during the week. On weekends we have a singer and trio who do mostly Cole Porter, Nöel Coward. A lot of our crowd were in the Hasty Pudding Club, and now and then one or two of them will give us a number. Lowell's one of our star performers. That's when it's really fun. Tell your Fox lady to come then. It's on the house, and have Lowell bring you."

"Well, thanks, I will. But you seem to be doing fine." Andy indicated the now almost full room. The noise and smoke were rising. Skip excused himself to greet a couple at the door.

"You all right, Andrea?" asked Lowell. "I didn't realize we were in for such a crowd. Sure you're okay? You look a little frazzled. Have another margarita. You need to unwind after working all weekend."

Was there an edge to his voice? No, she was tired, and she realized for the hundreth time that one thing she hated was trying to be social with a large gang she didn't really know—and if truth be told, didn't really like much. No, she was being unfair. She should be more outgoing. Lowell got up to confer with Skip, leaving Andy to face Vicky.

"Have you known Lowell a long time?" Andy asked, raising her voice above the hubbub.

"What?"

"I wondered how long you've known Lowell. Everyone here seems to know everybody."

"Oh, Lowell. I met him on Friday at Patti's bash. He's a doll, isn't he? Patti said he's engaged to some lady reporter who was out of town. I thought he seemed kind of upset the other night after a phone call. But then, later on, he got more relaxed." She lit a cigarette and looked over to where Lowell was standing, a faint smile on her bright, generous lips.

"You don't live here?"

"My family does, but I've been in New York since college. I'm with Wilhemina, the modeling agency, you know, but I came up to do a guest shot on "Spencer for Hire." It's a small part, but it could lead to other things. I can't go on being a hundred and twelve pounds and perfect forever."

Andy realized she hadn't noticed Vicky eating anything and that pink drink she was sipping was probably soda and a dash of cranberry juice, pale like the lamp shades. She belongs here, she thought, much more than I do. Was Lowell's annoyance at her for spending time with Tom Bradford a projection of his own somewhat roving eye? Oh, now stop being paranoid, she told herself. Suddenly she had a clear picture of Tom's face close to hers, his dark eyes clouded with yearning. She shut her eyes and slightly shook her head to clear the emotional image.

Lowell returned with a smile and more drinks. "How are you two lovelies getting on?"

"Uh, Lowell, I've really got to get going, so much to do tomorrow. Do you mind?"

"Not a bit, Andrea. I've got something on, too. He turned to bid Vicky farewell and shouted a general good-bye to those who could hear.

"That's better," he said, opening the car door, "We'll have a nightcap at The Lafayette."

"Well, I could use a coffee. All that smoke and talk makes me jumpy."

"Poor darling. I know it seems like a pretty closed club at first. It takes time to know them, but you'll really like them when you do, and they're bound to love you."

They drove in silence for a while. Why hadn't Lowell told Vicky they were engaged?

"Lowell, Vicky didn't seem to know about us. She said she'd heard you were engaged."

"Oh, well. I don't go around telling everyone I meet about us."

"I didn't think Vicky was just everyone. You must have had a good time Friday night."

"Well, when I decided to stop worrying about you and then imagining you and that Bradford guy together, I decided to unwind and enjoy."

"She looked like she enjoyed your unwinding."

"Andrea! You're jealous. Anyway, she's leaving for New York tomorrow."

After seating themselves at the comfortable Lafayette bar, Lowell ordered two stingers.

Andy teased, "Now what's the secret smile all about?"

"Ah, my plan, my pretty. While you were lolling about in the sun and spray, I was firming up a big deal with Whitney, Bancroft and Company. If I fly down to New York Wednesday, I should be able to meet with the chief stockholders and principals, wrap up the deal, and be back Saturday in time for our big bash."

"That seems pretty heavy. Why three days?"

"That's not long. Sometimes I'm gone a couple of weeks."

"Yes, but that's when you go overseas and not just before our engagement party. Well, all right. I guess I'll just have to survive."

"Sure you will, sweetie. I hope you're almost finished with that Bradford guy. My bank thinks he's bad news for our real estate section. We're pushing Sorley."

"Lowell, you're not! Sorley's a crook. You know that. Maybe he doesn't pull anything strictly illegal but he's out for all the big real estate interests and—" She stopped suddenly, realizing that the

Shamut Bank owned a considerable portion of Cape land.

Lowell looked at her keenly. "What is it, Andrea? You've been touchy all evening. What gives?"

"I don't know. Maybe it's these places. They're so damn fashionable and expensive. I'm just a simple person, I guess, with pretty simple tastes. If my dad could see me now, he'd think I was a kept woman."

"Ah, but you are, my darling. Pretty soon I'll be keeping you in furs and diamonds, everything your little heart desires."

"Oh, for God's sake, Lowell. You know I'm not the fur type, and I'd never wear diamonds in to work."

"Ah yes, work," said Lowell, "I was going to bring that up. Dad and Mother feel very strongly that after we're married, you'll just have to tell the *Tribune* good-bye. I'll be doing a lot of traveling, as you know, and I'll want you to come along and be my hostess, a helpmate. You know you can charm secrets out of a clam."

She couldn't believe her ears. "What are you saying, Lowell? Bottom line—are you saying you want me to give up my job, the column I've been struggling to get all my life, to be some kind of Mata Hari for you? I thought everyone understood that I'd go on working."

"For a time," he said. "For a time. But, Andrea darling, it just won't work for too long. I'll need you to help at important functions here and in—"

"Damn it, Lowell." Her patience ran out. "You can stuff your functions!" She gestured toward the bartender, who was staring questioningly at this unusual agitation. Her hand grazed Lowell's glass and knocked his stinger neatly into his lap.

"Oh, my God, I'm sorry," she wailed, "There I go again." She grabbed a tiny bar napkin and attempted to restore Lowell's trousers, much to his irritation. She whispered, "You see how great I'll be at your important functions. I'll probably smash someone's family heirloom and ruin you for life. Oh, Lowell, I'm so sorry."

Lowell ordered another drink and a temporary calm ensued.

"I thought it was all agreed that I'd keep my job. Pete thinks I'm really good, that I can even win a Pulitzer one day. Lowell dear, you can't seriously ask me to quit when I've just gotten started."

"Well," said Lowell, sipping delicately, "maybe I am being a little premature. I know it means a lot to you, Andrea, and I suppose you could stay on for a year or two. Maybe you could cover some of our Geneva meetings. You'll have to bone up on finance, of course."

"Thank you very much," she replied without warmth. "Speaking of boning up, tomorrow's Monday, and I've got some stuff to finish before I go in. Do you think we could leave now?"

Lowell gave her an odd look and asked for the bill. He paid and, to Andy's dismay, again left a very small tip. She must remember to ask him about that. Instead of departing by the street door, however, Lowell took her hand and entered the hotel's glittering lobby.

"Don't say anything, darling. I have a surprise."

Oh God, she thought, I'm too tired for any more surprises. He beckoned her into an elevator, pushed the button, and silently, they rose to the fifth floor.

"Lowell, what is all this?"

"You'll see."

She followed him down the thickly carpeted hall until they reached room 5-S. Producing a key, he opened the door with a flourish and ushered her into an exquisite sitting room where a bucketful of champagne sat dewily on a small table. To the right, an open door revealed a satin-covered double bed with the sheet turned down.

"Lowell, are you crazy? What is all this?"

"This, my little working girl, is a treat for both of us. My back is still suffering from the last night I spent on that torture chamber of yours you call a mattress. I mean it's been wonderful, but let's face it, you can't do much in a single bed but make out a little and try to sleep."

"Is that what we've been doing?" she asked. "Well, the next time you plan the Casanova act, I wish you'd warn me. It's beautiful, Lowell, but we'll just have to postpone it. I cannot be late to work with an unfinished assignment and a champagne hangover. Please understand. I just can't."

He grabbed her roughly, a new Lowell she hardly recognized. He kissed her with frenzy,

THE BEST MAN 163

forcing his mouth and teeth against hers while he forced his hand under her sweater to undo her bra. She twisted around, stumbling backward, laughing in embarrassment.

"Lowell honey, cut it out. Please. You don't have to ravish me. I'll come quietly, but not now, not tonight. I have to go home."

"Then I think you'd better hurry. Maybe I'll call up an old flame who'll be happy to share some good memories."

"Lowell, I know you're hurt, but don't say things you don't mean." She stooped to pick up her purse and left.

Was this the fun-loving, thoughtful, charming man she thought she knew? And loved? Like Scarlett, she'd think about that tomorrow. Right now she was really agitated. She hailed a cab and arrived gratefully at Linnean Street. Damn! Why did he have to pull that stuff tonight? Their timing was all off. She boiled a cup of instant coffee and forced herself to concentrate on fleshing out her notes into good journalese; the subject was Tom Bradford, candidate.

At one o'clock, more tired than she could remember being in a long time, she crawled into her "torture chamber" of a narrow bed and slipped into a light, troubled sleep.

That Monday, Andy seemed more preoccupied than usual. Pete even noticed but only asked if she were okay. He told her the piece she'd done on Tom Bradford had surpassed his expectations. The starchy candidate with good priorities but a lackluster personality suddenly emerged in her article as a man of genuine warmth, with a proud local and family background and even a dry sense of humor.

Andy had accurately portrayed his private persona, and she may have boosted his chances for the election. But Andy was conscious of a certain battle fatigue. She could use some time to herself, and she knew Lowell would need a day or two to forgive her and maybe himself.

Sure enough, he didn't call that evening. She kicked off her shoes and stuck a frozen dinner into the oven. She ate while watching a news show, then half-dozed through an old movie on the box. Just what I needed, she thought, stretching lazily. She even washed her hair.

The next day, surprisingly, Amy called and asked if they couldn't meet for a bite after work. She was having problems with her boyfriend, who had asked her to decorate his condo, hinting that she choose things she would like to live with. They shared a meal in Andy's flat, ordering Chinese—shrimp and sweet-and-sour pork. Sure enough, Lowell called, blithe as ever. He seemed truly disappointed to find her busy.

"You're sure it's sis you're with, Andrea darling? If I thought—" But at that moment Amy giggled, and he sounded mollified. "I hope you've gotten over our little misunderstanding. I only wanted to make us happy. Guess my timing wasn't too hot."

"That's okay, Lowell. My fault, too. I was too

tired to enjoy it. Next time I'll spend the day resting up for the night."

"Well, listen. I know you're working tomorrow. Damn shame, too, but let's get together for lunch. Don't forget I'm leaving for New York on the two-thirty shuttle."

"Sure, Lowell. I'll get Pete to let me out at twelve. But it'll have to be somewhere near."

"Right. I'll pick you up, and we'll get a bite at The Hilton Grill. See you then, Andrea."

Andy stared at the phone for a moment. Had she expected him to be more upset, more apologetic? Never mind. She and Amy finished their feast, and she shoved the big carton of uneaten takeout rice in the fridge.

"There's enough rice left over for three more meals. I always end up throwing it out weeks later. It makes me feel guilty."

"Oh, Andrea," laughed her sister. "Next thing, you'll be taking in stray dogs and cats. Lowell will love that."

"Okay, okay. Now tell me more about what's his name . . . Bill?"

Next morning, Andy dressed more carefully than usual. No trousers today. Finally, running ten minutes late, she opted for her short black skirt, yellow silk blouse, and white linen jacket. Pete would wonder, but let him.

"Hi, Andy. Hold it," he immediately ordered. "Those guys at the sewage plant are in for a thrill. What's the occasion?"

"Damn! I forgot. I thought that was Thursday. Do you think I can make it back by noon?"

"Oh, I get it. Glamour boy taking you to lunch?"

"Please, Pete. He's got a name. I wouldn't have said yes, but he's going to New York for three days, and we have to talk. You know the party's this Saturday. You haven't forgotten?"

"Wouldn't miss it. Gotta check out the competition."

"No competition with you, boss. I'm yours to command. Look, I'll make a few calls and get down to the plant. Let's hope I don't step in anything."

"If you do, you've got a hot exposé item. Either way, you win. See you later."

At eleven-fifty, still adequately pristine save for a few lineny creases, Andy returned to the office. Lowell was waiting.

"Well, well, I didn't know girl reporters were so dazzling on the job. You look like a daffodil."

"Yes and only slightly wilted. I'm famished. Let's see, spare ribs or a bacon burger. Maybe the London broil."

"Now I know why you love me, Andrea. I feed you. Maybe we should order steak tartare. They can start serving as we sit down."

"No kidding, Lowell, I must have walked five miles around that plant this morning. It's really amazingly clean for sewage disposal."

Lowell wrinkled his patrician nose and pretended to move away from her.

"Oh, come off it, Lowell. I washed my hands."

THE BEST MAN

He drove to the restaurant and they enjoyed a light, pleasant meal of spinach quiche and white wine, followed by double espressos. Isn't it silly, she thought—not for the first time—we get giddy for the first half hour and sober the next? Neither of them mentioned Sunday night.

Lowell was in full spate with strategies for the new game afoot among the corporate Tallyrands of New York's financial world. He would best them with a combination of daring and a carefully wrought prospectus for a new merger. We're so alike in some ways, she thought. Both so competitive. But he seems to enjoy the fame almost more than the result, and for me it's the result that matters.

He drove her back promptly at one-thirty, kissed her lightly, and promised to be back well ahead of the party. He pressed a tiny box into her hand, smiled, and drove off. She knew it was his grandmother's famous ring that she had jokingly promised to wear in twenty years. She could, she supposed, wear it just for the party and imagined it slipping off, never to be recovered. Oh, Lowell.

That evening, as she was kicking off her heels, the phone rang. Lowell, she guessed, but to her chagrin, she heard Tom Bradford's voice.

"Hi, Andy. It's Tom. Sorry I got my feathers ruffled last weekend. I guess I never wanted it to end. Can I buy you dinner and make up for my bad manners?"

"Well, Tom, I don't know, I . . ."

"Look, I'm only in town till Friday, and I've got

Thursday night free. You can ask me all about the upcoming debate in Brewster, a scoop for the *Trib*. Please, Andy."

He sounded so eager for company—her company. But she felt strange going to dinner with the man most likely to upset Lowell. Then the solution came. She flicked open her datebook and there was Thursday night, seven-thirty, Roby's play, with the tickets clipped to the page.

"Tell you what, Tom. I've got to work late tomorrow, but I've got two tickets to the opening of a new play at the Charles. I've been so busy, I'd forgotten till just this minute. Maybe you could meet me there, and we could grab a sandwich later."

"Perfect! I love going to plays and almost never have the time. See you then, Andy, and thanks."

Was she crazy? She had hoped to see Tom again after she was officially and publicly engaged. Then he would understand without her having to discuss it. Oh, well, it was just a play. Nothing very compromising there.

Thursday was beautiful. Bright sunlight invaded even the dark offices of the *Tribune*, causing an outbreak of spring fever on all sides. Brown bags meant for quick bites at the desk were taken out to sidewalk stoops and the grassy Common. Daffodils and the first tulips and the blush of cherry blossoms were everywhere. Andy found herself smiling for no reason. She heard her father's voice: *The first spring day is in the Devil's pay.* How strange. For once the memory brought her more pleasure than pain. Anyway, it wasn't the first spring day, but it had that feel.

She left work early. No one, including Pete, was feeling pressured. She showered, humming, "I ride an Ole Paint, I lead an Ole Dan—" Then the phone interrupted. She raced, dripping, to answer, feeling a sharp stab of disappointment. It would be Tom calling to say he couldn't make it. But it was her mother.

"Andrea darling, I've got your dress for the party. I've taken it in just a tad at the waist, but you'll have to try it on."

"Sure, Mom. But look, why don't I come a little earlier on Saturday, say five-thirty, and we can do everything then."

"Well, Amy will be here to make sure the musicians know their schedule. They've got some awful name like the Four Madcaps. She and Lowell have all these special numbers picked out."

"That's fine, but look, Mom, I've got to run. I'm catching the new play at the Charles. You know, the one with Lowell's brother Roby."

"That's nice, dear. I wonder if Margaret and Henry will be there? No, I suppose not."

"Right, Mom. See you Saturday. 'Bye."

She fixed a tuna fish sandwich and watched the local news. She was about to don her yellow silk blouse but rejected it. There was something faintly disloyal, wearing it so soon. The green paisley with her white jacket would do. Silver Moroccan earrings and bracelet. Yes, it would do nicely. Why was she being so fussy? She was only going into a dark theater with a man who was only a professional acquaintance. Oh, Andy, she thought, you know you want to look nice. He thinks you're pretty. Why disappoint him?

She spotted Tom from a distance. A parking place around the block had been suddenly freed just as she was beginning to panic. Oh, God! Seven-twenty-eight. He was looking worried, but his face lit up and he waved the second he spotted her racing through the traffic.

"Slow down, Andy. We've got time. They never go up exactly at seven-thirty. Probably waiting for Kevin Kelly. Say, you look wonderful. What a day, eh? Umm. You smell good, just like spring."

"It's Vent Vert," she said hurriedly.

"Green wind. It suits you."

He grasped her arm firmly as they pushed through the excited crowd. Andy recognized the producer, Frank Scanlon, beaming in the lobby. He stepped forward and greeted them with genuine enthusiasm.

"You've got my support, Mr. Bradford. Too bad we live just out of your district."

He smiled approvingly at Andy and clasped her hand with evident pleasure.

"I think this play's a winner. Of course, I always think that but more so this time. Nice to see you. Enjoy. Oh, there's an open bar at intermission."

They found their seats, fourth row center. The

THE BEST MAN 171

excitement was infectious. Finally, in the tense, sudden quiet, the curtain rose. The scene was a wild moorland in Scotland with clumps of heather among stones and bracken. There were purplish mountains in the back and a Gypsy caravan downstage right. Some children chased barefoot around the wagon and disappeared. Men's voices were heard in fierce argument. Then Andy recognized Roby dressed pretty much as she had last seen him on Chestnut Street. The other man was older, obviously the less hot-headed of the two.

Apparently a government agency had delivered an ultimatum. Either they send their children to the local public school or they would be removed to foster homes. Roby's character was adamant. He would fight them, shoot if necessary. Hadn't they always educated their kids in what they needed to know? He was teaching them to read and do sums. What else was necessary? His comrade was just as pained as Roby, but knew that change was inevitable. Hadn't they all been fingerprinted at the local constabulary? They had felt the shame of it, but the danger was too great. It was go with the changes or lose their children. Perhaps forever.

In the following scene, a young woman from town arrived to try to convince the Gypsy women of the county's good intentions. She was charmed by the handiwork she saw, by the children themselves, and their imaginative games. She began to doubt her own superiors. Or was she being too subjective, too sentimental? And have they laid this on just to impress her? Roby entered and told her she wasn't wanted. What did she know about their lives? He made fun of her outfit, of her shoes, and said she wouldn't last in their way of life for a week. She was furious but obviously attracted. She told him she'd prove him wrong. She'd come on Saturday to spend the week, then make her report. Roby laughed jeeringly and walked out.

At intermission, Tom and Andy were both enthusiastic.

"I had a little trouble with the accents at first," he confessed, "but when you get used to it, it's great. Can I get ye a wee dram o' whiskey, lass?"

"Hey, Tom, that's good. As a Ferguson, I had plenty of Robert Burns in my young life, courtesy of Dad. He had a great burr when he did 'wee sleekit cowerin timerous beastie.' Yow don't know the one, do you?"

"Oh, yes. 'I wish that God the gift had gi us, to see ourselves as others see us.'"

"You know that?"

"Yes." He smiled warmly. "Two Scotches, please."

"This should really put us in the mood. I had a sandwich before, thank goodness."

They downed their drams and hurried back to their seats.

"You want to bet he falls for her?" whispered Tom.

"No bet. But do they end up together?"

At that moment, the curtain rose, revealing a

moonlit heath and a campfire surrounded by several Gypsies and Fiona Aiken, the government girl, now clad in jeans and a flowered shirt and vest. The talk was muted. Only a few weeks remained before they either leave or agree to submit. A woman recited the old Gypsy chant about the wind that grows stale in closed rooms, that worldly goods possess the soul and love is a blowing wind opening hearts and minds.

Someone passed a bottle around and Roby entered, glanced at Fiona, and took his place across from her. A guitar was produced and one of the girls asked Roby to play. He hummed and stroked the instrument. Suddenly his clear tenor voice rose in the bittersweet old song, "The Black-eyed Gypsy."

Andy listened to the lyric that spoke of sleeping in the arms of the black-eyed Gypsy, and the image of Tom's dark eyes appeared in her mind. With the lilting melody, she could almost feel his sure, comforting arms around her. Then she heard the most poignant lines....

> No, I won't take off my high-heeled boots
> Nor my gloves of Spanish leather oh
> For I'd rather one kiss from the Gypsy's lips
> Than all of your land and money oh
> Than all of your land and money oh.

He was still singing. Andy felt tears in her eyes and suddenly Tom's hand touched hers. It was only for a moment, a shared moment of beauty and feeling, but that moment was enough to unseal all her resolutions, her half-formed plans for the future. She felt warmth and electricity in her blood. Was it Tom? She felt suddenly released from all her past and at the same time, she was at peace with it. She was flooded by memories of nights at the ranch and the old joy she'd thought she'd lost forever with Ben's passing. She felt shaken and exalted. Tears ran down her cheeks, and she didn't care. Tom noticed and this time took her hand and kept it in his. She didn't stir.

She couldn't seem to concentrate on the rest of the play although it was no fault of the story or the actors. Fiona's city suitor had confronted Roby, who, rather than spend time in jail, elected to join comrades in Ireland, leaving Fiona forlorn but wiser. The Gypsy camp was broken up, and disgruntled families prepared to move into the town, at least for the winter. Finally, they all joined in, singing "The Traveling People."

The curtain slowly fell after several company bows. Andy and Tom sat as the audience made its way noisily out. By now, she was in control.

"I loved it. All right, so it was a little sentimental maybe, but wasn't Roby wonderful? What a voice!"

"I don't mind sentiment," said Tom in a subdued voice, "when it's based on real feeling. You know, Andy, I see people being wrenched out of their old lives all the time, people who made good money once and can't afford to support their families when the mills close or the fishing dries up—more and more homeless, not enough federal money. There are even the ones who'd rather live on the streets than in some lousy welfare hotel, but children need homes and schools. I guess I could identify with both sides...."

He rose and stretched his long body, then reached down to help Andy with her jacket. "Would you like to get a bite?"

"There's someone I have to see, Tom, the one who gave me the tickets—Roby."

"Why didn't you tell me you knew him? He's terrific. I'd like to get him singing at some of our rallies. He can really move people." They steered their way through the crowd of enthusiastic fans. Andy gave Roby a big hug and, after a moment's hesitation, he hugged her in return.

"You liked it, huh? I figured you might. Is Lowell here? Or couldn't he make it?"

"No, uh, he had a very important conference in New York but he sent you his best," she lied. She supposed Lowell had forgotten about it as she almost had. "This is Tom Bradford. I'm covering his campaign for the *Trib*."

"Oh, sure. Glad you could make it."

"Thank Miss Ferguson. She had an extra seat. I really liked the play but especially your songs. I'd like to call you if I may about doing some TV spots with me when the campaign starts heating up."

"Sure, love to. Sorley is a frightening individual. Give me a call."

"Right. Thanks again."

" 'Bye, Roby. I'll get Lowell to come another time."

"Who's this Lowell?" asked Tom as they made their way toward the exit, but a woman in a hurry forced her way between them at that moment, and Andy's mumbled reply was lost.

"Are you hungry?" he asked.

"Not anymore, Tom. As a matter of fact, I'm very nicely tired. The play really drained me. I want to think about it."

She wanted to think about a whole lot more than the play. She could still feel her hand in his, see his dark, Gypsy eyes.

"Well, let me drive home with you, and I'll walk to my place from there. Linneaen, isn't it? Not that far."

She agreed, and they drove quietly home. He walked her to her apartment entrance and as he bent down to kiss her, she stepped back and gently touched his cheek.

"Thanks, Tom," she whispered. Despite his expression of puzzled yearning, she firmly closed the door. Then she stood waiting for him to go. "Please, please leave," she prayed softly, "before I make a fool of myself—if I haven't already."

Finally she heard his reluctant steps turn toward the street. She felt like sinking to her knees with relief, but she managed to climb the stairs to her apartment and move to her small bedroom before flopping across the bed in a state of emotional confusion.

What are you doing, Andy Ferguson? You are

going to be Mrs. Lowell Curtis. By next week the whole of Boston will know it. Oh, God, Tom will know it. Hell and damnation. Now he'll hate me.

She wept and raged until she felt calm enough to shuck off her rumpled dress and fix a cup of soup. Tomorrow was Friday. She would ask Pete to take her off the assignment, at least temporarily. No, it could wait until Monday. So much to do. Her eye fell on the tiny box concealing the immense ring. Oh, God, Lowell and the engagement party! She would see it through—but *without* the burden of his grandmother's diamonds.

NINE

THE SHRILL ALARM clock woke Andy with a start. She'd tossed and turned all night. And her restless sleep wasn't just because of the evening with Tom, but the ill-timed phone call she'd gotten late last night from Lowell....

"Hi, beautiful. I'm back. The deal went perfectly with Whitney, Bancroft. Bancroft took a little persuading but I sent his wife, Lucy, a baby bauble from Cartier. The bank footed the tab, of course. After that, everything went swimmingly. Sorry I didn't have time to call my snowbird these past three days, but all my time was taken up being Mr. Charming, and it sure paid off.

"Tomorrow's our big do at your mother's and I'm rarin' to go," he continued. "I did ask a few more of my buddies. One guy from the bank. Oh, and I happened to run into Vicky at Doubles on Thursday night, so I told her to pop over to Newton on Saturday."

"I'm glad you're back, Lowell. I've got a lot to do before the party, so I'll see you at six at Mom's."

"Is that all you have to say? That's not like you, an opinion on everything."

"That's all for now, Lowell. See you later," said Andy, and slammed down the phone.

What was Lowell doing at Doubles? Where did he get the time to go dancing during a business trip? Was it just coincidence that Vicky was there?

On the other hand, while Lowell was with Vicky, she was with Tom listening to "The Black-eyed Gypsy." That haunting refrain had been beating in her head all night. "I'd rather one kiss from the Gypsy's lips than all your land and money." Maybe that's why she'd had such an awful night. She just couldn't shut out all the doubts that were swimming around in her head.

She thought of Lowell. They'd had just one superficial lunch after that Lafayette debacle, and he'd said nothing about his behavior. Absolutely nothing! But that's how Lowell was. To the outside world, everything was glorious. Andy wished they'd had just one night to make everything right again in her head before the engagement party, but there wasn't time. Maybe, she admitted, there'd never be enough time. No, she was better off thinking about how it had been early on with Lowell. That's what seems to have been lost: Her shining, charming, magnetic Lowell.

The phone rang again. "Good morning, Andrea, darling. No spring showers today. Aren't we lucky?" It was Grace and she never sounded merrier.

"We sure are, Mom. I'm glad you and Amy have everything under control." No guts, Andy Ferguson. Why not tell your mother you're all confused and this whole thing was beginning to seem like a sham? Nope, you've made up your mind, onward and upward, no turning back.

"They're putting up the tent right now," said Grace. "Amy's thrilled because it's a three-poler."

"What in the world does that mean?"

Grace laughed. "Oh, Andrea. You just never were the party girl. It means the tent needs three center poles to hold it up. It takes up practically the whole backyard. Do you think we should have pink and white ribbons, or just white on the poles? That's what I wanted to know."

Andy's mind flashed back to Amy's graduation. She'd had the graduation party, of course, and it had taken all Ben's persuasion to talk Grace out of having a tent. "If it rains, they should wear slickers and umbrellas," he'd said. "Tents are for camping and circuses." That's what this engagement party was turning into. A three-ring, three-pole circus.

"Whatever you and Amy decide is fine for me. I'm not exactly the ribbon type."

"Well, it's all thrilling. I've even gotten some phone calls from the Johnsons and Morgans asking where you've registered. I told them only Shreve's."

"I've never met the Johnsons and Morgans," said Andy.

"Well, dear. They're intimate friends of the Curtises. Will you be over here at five to try on the dress?"

Dress! She wouldn't mind Pete's giving her an assignment in Australia right now. Instead, she was about to try on some yellow-flowered dress that Grace said was just perfect. "Sure, Mom, see you at five."

Even though it was Saturday, Andy decided to go into the office. "There's nothing like good exercise and hard work to take your mind off things," Ben had always said. And he had practiced what he preached. Chopping logs at the ranch, cleaning his horses, building a one-room cabin himself. "My escape hatch from my escape," he'd called it. And then there was his beloved Timberline Press. He proofed every word, monitored the printing late at night. He missed a lot of parties that way. He'd found a way to survive. But was Ben Ferguson a happy man when he wasn't on the ranch, working, or with his beloved Andy? She'd never really thought about that and now there was so much to think about ... too much.

Andy jogged along the Charles River for an hour. The breezes felt cool and soft but did not help her muddled head. She drove to the office in her sweats and running shoes. Hardly anyone would be there Saturday at noon. She'd finish up a soft piece she was writing on Mahoney's Rocky Ledge—the twenty-acre, twenty-million-dollar nursery business in Winchester. "Pete, writing about twenty thousand gardeners buying fertilizer just isn't my bag," she'd told him.

"It'll take your mind off the Sorley-Bradford campaign. There will be a lot of fertilizer slung around in that one," said Pete.

She was glad now that she had nothing more controversial to write about than mulch and magnolias. As always, when she concentrated on her copy, the two hours sped by. There was no time to think about three-polers or how many of Lowell's Beachcomber friends would show . . . or even Tom Bradford's haunting eyes.

It was five-fifteen when she turned her VW Rabbit onto her mother's street. She was fifteen minutes late—not bad for her. She'd tossed on a T-shirt and blue jeans. Her sling-back imitation Chanel shoes seemed a bit incongruous on her feet, but soon she'd be slipping into her engagement-party dress that Grace had in readiness. Andy knew Grace would never have trusted her to drive over in it. "You'd spill something for sure!" That's what Grace would have said if Andy'd put up any fuss.

As Andy pulled the car into the driveway, behind three pink trucks with PERFECT PALATE PARTY PLANNERS splashed on the sides, she saw a white canopy leading up the brick walk to the front door. Damn. This wasn't a wedding. What had Grace told the Curtises the night of the "summit meeting"? "We're having just an *informal* engagement party." Baloney. Andy should have known better.

Andy walked unsteadily to the front door, partly because she knew she wasn't going to like what she saw when she opened it, but mostly because her fake Chanels were too tight. There, standing in the doorway was Grace Ferguson, in a diaphanous pink chiffon, Amy in a skin-tight rose silk sheath that revealed every curve, and an older woman in a black uniform with a starched white apron.

"Maureen, what are you doing here?" asked an astonished Andy.

"Margaret Curtis thought Maureen would add a special touch. Just like the Parkers," said Grace.

"Who are the Parkers?" demanded Andy. "I've never heard of any Parkers."

"The men I've hired to park all the cars, dear. Otherwise there'd be an absolute traffic jam."

"Come on, Andrea, don't be an old prune face," chirped Amy. "Mom and I have been working like beavers. Wait until you see what it looks like under the tent. Perfect Palate Party Planners has put Newport to shame. Tina Buffington, eat your heart out."

"Run upstairs, dear, and put your dress on," said Grace. "The folds ought to be just right over your nice, slim hips. Anybody would give their eyeteeth to have your figure."

Andy's dress lay on the unfamiliar lavender quilt in the room that was her mother's—her father wouldn't have stayed for five minutes in this room, with its chintzed chaise longue and mirrored dressing table with matching fabric skirt. She lifted the dress—yellow-flowered silk with a boat neck, simply belted. It suited her. Andy felt she'd been unfair to her mother.

On top of the dress was a small box wrapped in pink tissue paper and white ribbons. Andy slowly opened the package. Inside was a strand of pearls, small yet perfectly matched. Andy, who never noticed jewelry, vaguely remembered her mother wearing these sometime long ago in Denver. On white note paper with a scrolled G.L.F. at the top was written, *Your father gave me these pearls when we were engaged. I know he would want them to be yours.* Andy sat on the bed, put her head in her hands, and sobbed. What a sweet gesture on her mother's part, and yet she felt she was being swept out to sea in a tidal wave. She wanted to go on a pack trip with her father like the one the two of them took high in the Rockies when she was debating whether or not to accept her scholarship to Columbia School of Journalism.

"It's a time of new beginnings," said Ben, piling a hunk of cheddar on some sourdough bread he'd baked at the ranch. "I'll miss you. Don't look back, though," he laughed. "Somebody might be following you, and it'd be me. Just full speed ahead. Take charge of your life."

That's what I'm going to do, she thought. If only I'd had some time with Lowell after that disastrous Sunday. That superficial lunch didn't accomplish anything.

"Andy dear, are you ready? I want to show you the tent before anybody comes. Lowell called and said he'd pick up Margaret and Henry and be here at six-thirty."

Andy tossed off her jeans, slipped into the tailored yellow dress, and clasped the sentimental pearls around her neck. She felt strange wearing jewelry, but these pearls were different. She realized more and more how much a part of her Ben would always be.

"Coming, Mom." Andy joined Grace and Amy in the front hall. She leaned over and gave her Mother a kiss. "Thank you for the pearls. I'll treasure them."

"Well, you always were Daddy's girl. Now, Amy, you lead the way."

Amy, high-heeled silver sandals clicking, led Andy and Grace through the living room. There were large containers of rubrum lilies on the side tables, and Andy noticed that the ersatz Georgian mantel was banked in greens and clusters of the same lilies. Then Grace flung open the doors to the back, previously a plain old yard with room for a Weber grill and a redwood picnic table. Andy gasped. It was as if the Wicked Witch of the North had waved her wand and transformed 121 Pleasant Street into everything Andy hated. A pink tent covered the entire area. There were three center poles and ten poles on each side holding up the canopy. Each pole was twisted with garlands of ivy and lilies; pink and white ribbons floated from the top downward. At one end of the tent was a wooden dance floor.

A dance floor, thought Andy, and me with shoes that hurt already. Tables for eight with white chairs were scattered about. Each was covered with a pink, round linen cloth, violet-flowered napkins fanned out at each place, and votive lights twinkled around small baskets of lilies.

Oh, my God, thought Andy. This is strictly the Hamptons, Newport, and Watch Hill rolled into one. It reeks with chic. Would *Town and Country* be covering this event, or had Grace lined up the *New York Times*? Lowell would probably love it all. Andy rolled a curl around her forefinger. Mom's gone to all this trouble, and I'm miserable. I'll be a clod on the dance floor. I'll embarrass Lowell. Do I care if I embarrass Lowell? Maybe his snow maiden is turning to ice. Amy's overcheery voice jolted Andy out of her musings.

"Isn't this just fab, Andrea? Mom and I have been working on this for days. The votive lights were Mom's idea, but the maypole effect was mine. It's just perfect, isn't it? I almost feel like this is my engagement party, not yours."

Andy wanted to take her little sibling and strangle her in the pink and white ribbons. Instead she said, "Amy. It couldn't be prettier. I just wish you'd use your talents to be a top interior designer. You'd be wonderful. I could never dream up any of this. You know me. I'm much more comfortable in jeans writing about a construction gang kickback."

"I know that, Andrea. But that's not what Lowell's going to want," said Amy, whipping out a cigarette from a minuscule silver bag that snapped onto her belt. "Here. Do you want a drag?" she asked.

"If I want anything right now, it's a belt of Scotch," said Andy.

"Not before we have the first dance, gorgeous," said a familiar voice behind her. Andy wheeled to face Lowell in a blue pinstripe suit, followed by Margaret and Henry Curtis.

"Hope I can have the second," piped in Amy.

"No, the second goes to my mother, then let the chips fall where they may," said Lowell. He gave Margaret Curtis a peck on the cheek and then walked up to Grace and put his arm around her.

"You're looking wonderful, Grace. You, too, Amy. It's all a mighty purty family I'm getting hitched up with," Lowell drawled exaggeratedly.

Andy shuddered at the words "mighty purty." Any slight ridicule of the West and her beloved Colorado made her blood boil.

"Who's the band, Andrea?" asked Lowell. "I just thought you'd like to know, I've got on my dancing shoes."

"Amy picked the band. I didn't even ask."

"It's the Four Hubcaps, Lowell," said Amy. "Tina tells me they're going to be big on the deb circuit this June."

"Is that so?" Margaret asked, looking at Lowell.

"Well, I have heard of them, Mother. I promise you, they're the *in* trio. Skip was thinking of having them on Wednesdays at The Beachcomber."

"Well, then I think they're charming," said Mrs. Curtis.

Lowell smiled, and Andy noticed again how similar his smile was to his mother's. His eyes, which usually didn't light up, shone in a unique way when he looked at her. Had this always bothered Andy or was this just the first time?

"They'll all love seeing you, too, Mother," he said. Then, almost as an afterthought, he said, "And you, too, my pretty. The girl of my dreams."

Why does he have to keep saying such trite things? thought Andy. His clients might go for this but I just don't.

"Hey, kid, where's the bar?" The familiar voice of Pete rang out, and Andy smiled. Pete and Gabe had arrived together, of course. The first. They both wore slightly rumpled suits, neckties askew. Andy was amazed they had on neckties at all. She felt bolstered by their presence.

"Over there," said Andy, pointing to a long banquet table way to one side of the tent, covered with a pink cloth and enough bottles to fill a state liquor store. "Come on, I'll take you over."

"Aren't you going to introduce me?" said Lowell as he walked over to Pete and Gabe, handsomer and more self-assured than ever.

"I'm the lucky man, here," he said. He shook hands with both of them and glanced at the third finger of Andy's left hand. Andy watched his face. There was no change of expression, there never was when Lowell was really irritated, but she knew he noticed she wasn't wearing his grandmother's engagement ring.

"Hi, Lowell. Boy, this has the look of a real bash." It was Vicky, raven-haired Vicky in a blue-sequinned jumpsuit. She was flanked by Jilly and Skip. Jilly's hair was flattened by a silver band and her stomach by silver pants two sizes too small. Skip had on a khaki suit and yellow shirt. Loafered and sockless, he was the perfect preppy.

"Sandy and Patti are on their way, and Ivor's just smoothing down his balding pate," said Skip. "The whole gang will be here, Lowell. After all, you're the first one to leave us."

"I'm not going anywhere," said Lowell. "I'm just bringing another bird into our flock."

Andy, who felt like a librarian in her proper tailored dress and squeaky shoes, was only too glad to escape to the bar with Pete and Gabe, but not before she noticed Amy making a bee line for Ivor, who had just sauntered in.

"Some fancy goings-on, Andy," said Gabe, "I guess I just never pictured you in such a scene."

"Come on, Gabe," said Pete. "Andy can handle everything. I must say Lowell comes off as quite the golden boy."

Andy looked over her shoulder to see the golden boy totally surrounded. More and more people were streaming in. She recognized Amy's friend, Tina, and husband Lucien, who seemed to blend in perfectly. Grace was saying hello to a few friends Andy didn't know.

Waitresses in black pants, vests, and bow ties appeared as if out of a genie bottle. They all carried silver trays. Some had mushrooms stuffed with crabmeat and endives filled with Roquefort cheese. Others had a base of alfalfa sprouts heaped with sliced potatoes laced with a dollop of sour cream and black or red caviar.

"Perfect Palate Catering is going to retire on this one," said Pete.

"Trust you to notice those awful pink trucks," said Andy.

"I'm not city editor for nothing, Andy. Come on, I want a Scotch. Don't you?"

"I sure do, but I'd fall flat on my face. Pete, I just wish we were at Perry's having those stale pizzas with exhausted anchovies and a pitcher of beer."

"I bet you do. You'd better go over to your fiancé or you'll give your mother heart palpitations. Don't forget. I'm not going anywhere. When you need a plank to go ashore on, just whistle. That is, if you can hear me above that band's racket."

Barry and the boys had started playing at full volume. Amy and Ivor were wiggling to the disco beat. In fact, the dance floor was already full. It looked like a recreation of The Beachcomber. Andy didn't seem to know any of these people. But Amy was in her element. She noticed Andy standing like a forlorn waif and dragged Ivor off the dance floor.

"I guess I made a mistake, Andrea," said Amy, and Andy could tell she was sincere. "This is certainly more my scene than yours, but go grab your guy. Then you'll have fun, too. I promise. There he is at that first table by the dance floor."

Andy looked toward the table, and there he was, indeed. A margarita in one hand and Vicky on his lap. Andy approached slowly.

"Just because I'm tying the knot in June doesn't mean it's the end of everything," Lowell was saying to Vicky, who took the margarita out of his hand and started drinking it.

"Here's to you, gorgeous," she said as Andy walked up. Lowell didn't seem the slightest bit dismayed. As always, he had an answer for everything.

"Hi, snow maiden. Just kissing my girls goodbye. Hop down now, Vicky, and go play in the traffic."

Andy could tell Lowell, despite his predictable outward composure, was well into the margaritas. He rose, swaying a bit, and took Andy's hand. "Come on, Andrea, let's do some dirty dancing." He started pulling her toward the dance floor.

"Lowell," said Andy, "You know I'm not much of a dancer. Besides which, my shoes hurt."

"Shoes," said Lowell. "Who needs shoes? They're just for drinking champagne." He sat Andy on the edge of the dance floor and tugged off her fake Chanels.

This is mad, thought Andy as she watched Lowell grab a glass of champagne from a tittering woman in gold-sequined pants and a black see-through blouse. He poured the wine into one of Andy's shoes. Then as Lowell put a shoe to his lips, the liquid slid out of the sling-back all over his blue pinstripe suit. Andy had never seen Lowell disheveled. And she'd never seen him really drunk. She looked at Amy, so happy twisting and turning with Ivor, who was balancing a beer bottle on his head. Somebody was a fish out of water here. Guess who?

Andy watched as Patti Somebody, one of The Beachcomber gang, moved in. "Hey, Lowell," said Patti, "let me mop you up a bit. Then how about a farewell whirl? It's the shank of the evening. You don't mind, do you, Andrea? After all, this is his last fling. Ha-ha."

Lowell never gave Andy a chance to answer. He took off like a shot to cavort with Patti, waving his jacket like a matador while Patti pretended to be the bull.

"It's always going to be like this, you know, Gypsy woman," said a familiar voice. It was Roby. In his blue jeans, boots, and Mexican shirt, he was the most welcome sight Andy had seen since Pete and Gabe had slouched in.

"Roby," said Andy. "Am I glad to see you. I didn't know you were going to be here, but then, I didn't know a lot of these guests. It's a surprise party, that's what it is."

"Mother seems to be having a fine time. My brother can do no wrong in her eyes."

Andy noted a hint of bitterness in Roby's voice, but she was having too many problems of her own right now to help him out.

"My mother's enjoying herself, too," said Andy. "I'm glad she is. This all means a lot to her. She's always dreamed of having a party like this, though I'm sure she thought it would be for Amy, not for me."

"You're a little like me, aren't you, Andy?" said Roby. "I don't mean that you're an outcast, but you sure are an iconoclast."

Andy realized that Roby was the only one, except for the *Trib* gang and her father, who called her "Andy." Oh, and Tom Bradford. Tom had never called her anything else ever since the first time they met in his office. That was before the weekend in Truro, before the play, before her world had been turned topsy-turvy. But it was *this* sphere that seemed upside down to her. Tom's world made perfect sense. It was as if she'd stepped through the looking glass. Here she was at her own mad tea party led by the Four Hubcaps.

"I'd love to have you sing here, right now, but I know it's not the time or the place. You have a remarkable talent, Roby. I just hope that I'll be able to achieve as much in my writing. Pete over there, the big guy leaning on the bar, has taken me under his wing. He's given me a real opportunity. First my own column and now the series I'm doing on Tom Bradford."

"You and Tom certainly seemed in tune Thursday night at my play."

"Well, Lowell was in New York, and you had given me those comps. I hated to have them go to waste, and I'm doing this big political assignment—" Andy had started to rush her words and wave her arms.

"Calm down, Andy. You'll soon be in my family, and I'm damn glad. You're the best thing that's ever happened to it. I just hope Lowell realizes what a lucky guy he is. But I'm no fool. I couldn't help thinking it wasn't just me who had that effect on you when you came backstage. Tom Bradford seemed a bit shaken, too."

"Did I hear the name Tom Bradford?" Andy and Roby looked up as a tall man in a gray herringbone jacket and gray flannels leaned over them. He was so all together that Andy tried to tuck her shoeless feet under her ... ? What had Lowell done with her new shoes anyway?

"Let me introduce myself. My name is Alec Cheever."

"Time for my exit, Andy," said Roby. "I'm going to blow this joint. Nice to have met you, Mr. Cheever. See you from the stage, Andy." Then Roby wended his way through the twinkling candles, the Perfect Palate waitresses, the jumpsuits, and flowered minis until Andy lost sight of him.

"I've been wanting to meet you, Andrea. I'm a very good friend of Lowell's and a colleague besides." said Alec.

"Hi," said Andy, wondering why Lowell had never mentioned him if he was such a good friend. The man was attractive, in a proper sort of a way. And for some reason she couldn't put her finger on, he reminded her of Tom's helper, Chip Bowman.

"I work at the Shamut Bank with Lowell. When

I heard you mention our arch-enemy, I just had to move in."

"What arch-enemy?" said Andy.

"Why, Tom Bradford. I'm sure you knew the bank was backing Gene Sorley. Lowell's given a large donation. Not his own bucks, but the bank's. I'm Gene Sorley's campaign manager. I know your paper's backing Bradford, but I'm sure you personally, being Lowell's fiancée, are on *our* team. Actually, Lowell was hoping Gene could put in a brief appearance here, but he's stuck in Dorchester. He's trying to assure the voters there he won't take away their low-income housing when he puts up his condos. But enough politicking. Shall we dance?"

Gene Sorley's campaign manager, thought Andy. At *my* party. Andy was stunned. She looked at Pete, who was ogling a pink chiffon balloon skirt. At least he had no idea who she was talking to. How could Lowell do this? He knew her paper was backing Tom Bradford. He knew how she felt about protecting the seashore's natural environment. But was that all he knew?

Andy needed to talk to Lowell. Right now— alone. She found her wet shoes sitting in the middle of the centerpiece on the table in front of her. She squeezed into them and wobbled over to her mother, who was seated, beaming, between Margaret and Henry Curtis.

"Andrea dear, isn't this terrific?" said Grace.

"It's beautiful, Mother. I know how much thought you put into every detail. It shows."

"Yes, Andrea," added Mrs. Curtis. "Your mother

has given a sensational party. You have an excellent teacher. I'm delighted. You and Lowell will be doing a lot of entertaining. He loves to, you know. We used to do so much in my younger days."

"Have you seen Lowell, Mrs. Curtis?"

"Certainly, he and that girl Vicky are up there with the Four Hubcaps."

"Thanks."

Andy walked slowly toward the gyrating mob, her feet hurting more than ever. A short woman with frizzy blond hair ran up to her. "Come on, bridie, let's shake, rattle, and roll. What a bash. I'm having the after-party party. Lowell's beginning to round up all the usual suspects. Oh, I don't know if we've actually met. I'm Buffy."

"Hi, Buffy. I guess you guys party nonstop."

"Well, Lowell's the first to do the ring thing, and we all want to give him a big send-off. Are you lucky. I know a lot of girls who wanted to get their claws into him."

Andy winced at that last remark.

"What's this? Someone taking my name in vain?" Lowell, abandoning a perturbed Vicky, approached Andy.

"Let's have one dance together, beautiful. It seems I haven't seen you all evening."

"Lowell, I want to talk," said Andy.

"We've got all our lives for that. Come on. Don't spoil everything."

"I don't think Andy's big on dancing. The Hubcaps were really my idea," said a welcoming voice.

Andy could hardly believe it. It was Amy to her rescue.

"Lowell's had too many margaritas," Amy whispered to Andy as she unwound herself from Ivor. "He'll be okay in the morning."

"Nothing will ever be okay in the morning, Amy," said Andy.

"Uh-oh. I remember that voice from long ago," said Amy. "Whatever you do, don't make a scene. Mother'd have a fit."

Andy remembered Ben's saying, "Your mother's big on appearances, Andy. It's not worth the bother to fight. Just let her have her way." I'll let Mother have her perfect party, thought Andy. But I don't think she'll like the grand finale. Well, here goes.

"Lowell," said Andy, "let's go sit at that table way in the corner, just for a minute."

Then Andy looked at Lowell. And the realization hit her, right between her own Gypsy eyes. He still had his winning smile, his worldliness, his charm—even when drunk. But she knew now that the two of them would never be a winning combination. There would always be a Vicky, there would always be a Gene Sorley campaign she disagreed with, there would always be this world—his world—in which she'd forever be a stranger. She wanted the dunes of Truro, the piercing moan of waves breaking. She wanted *Tom*. But that would take time. Lots of time.

"Lowell," she said firmly. "This just isn't working out."

Lowell put his arms around her waist and kissed

her hard on the lips. "I'm just trying to mend a few broken hearts before we take off," he said. "Don't get pouty, though you look awfully pretty when you're mad."

"Lowell," said Andy. "I'm going home."

"Can't do that, Andrea. Buffy's bash will be getting under way in about an hour."

"Lowell," said Andy calmly, and with more resolution than she'd had in two months. "I'm not going with you. Not now. Not ever. I'm going home—alone."

Lowell looked at Andy, smiled, and did not change expression. "See you in the morning, snow maiden," he said.

Andy walked over to Pete, who had not left the bar all night. "Pete," she said, "will you take me home? My feet are killing me."

"That's not all that's killing you. Let's go."

Once inside Pete's old Chevy, the floodgates opened. "Pete, this is all wrong. I can't live a banker's life, filled with parties and pinstripe politics. Lowell's just not for me. I tried to tell him, but I don't think he understands that a person like me would turn down a Lowell Gardner Curtis. God, Pete. What will my mother say?"

"It's your life, kid," said Pete as he drove up to Linneaen Street. "I think I know what Ben Ferguson would say: 'Make the choice you have to, then full speed ahead.' "

"Thanks, Pete," said a sniffing Andy before she jumped out of the car, shoes in hand, and ran barefoot up four flights of stairs to her apartment. The phone was ringing as she unlocked the door.

THE BEST MAN 199

She didn't answer it. Instead she tore off her dress, showered and pulled on jeans and an old blue workshirt. Knowing she had a lot to think about, she fixed a cup of hot chocolate and settled onto her couch, ignoring the phone a second time. She never felt freer.

TEN

Andy woke late Sunday morning with the realization that she must call her mother and explain all. After three cups of coffee and much delaying, she forced herself to dial Grace's number. The phone rang four times. Thank God, maybe she wasn't home . . .

"Yes? This is the Ferguson residence."

"It's Andy, Mom. I've got to talk to you. Something's happened . . . I can't marry Lowell."

"Andrea sweetheart, you're just having a bad case of pre-nuptial nerves. Come over here right now, and we'll talk."

The thought of explaining her decision face to face to her mother seemed impossible. It would surely end in an awful fight.

"I'm serious, Mom. I'm really having my doubts

about the wedding. I want to call the whole thing off. Honestly, Mom, I know it sounds crazy and all that, but I can't go through with it." There was a ghastly pause.

"You'd better get over here right now," said the icy voice, and the phone went dead. Maybe a hurricane would occur. Hurricane Andrea. Maybe she could get run over and bust a rib or two. Maybe the bank would send Lowell on a sudden secret mission, and he'd be gone for a couple of years— stop it, Andy! Her head whirled in dismay. She felt like Mary of Scotland walking toward the block as she climbed into her VW and started toward Newton.

She had already told Lowell it wasn't going to work. She couldn't marry him. She knew that now with absolute certainty. How had she ever imagined she could live in such opulence, spending evenings at The Beachcomber, attending the opera, which she always fell asleep at anyway? When could she work? And how could she cover assignments in south Boston among drug addicts, the poor, or even the middle class if they knew she was Mrs. Lowell Curtis—if *she* knew she was Mrs. Lowell Curtis? She still cared for him, of course. She felt a twinge of rueful pain at the memory of his fine, muscular body, his chiseled, tanned features, his quick laugh, their intense games, and elegant suppers. Yes, she almost had it all.... A memory of a weekend on the ranch returned to her. She was preparing to go to New York, having won her scholarship and was riding high....

"Do you think I can have everything, Daddy, the whole enchilada, the whole ball of wax?"

She was partly kidding, partly serious.

"What kind of slick magazine crap is that?" Ben had answered roughly. "Don't you know, honey, that 'everything' is nothing? Growing up means you choose a few things that are really important—what you believe, what you want to do, who you love. All that other stuff—the house, the car, the career and the kids, endless love, fame and parties—that's baloney. You have to make choices in work and love, and they both come from what you believe in. You're my girl, Andy, and I know you'll end up okay, but don't let me hear any more crap about enchiladas, even though I love 'em . . ."

Her mind was beginning to clear. She would always be grateful to Lowell, she thought, for the chance at "everything" because now she knew well that it wasn't for her.

She pulled the little red car up in front of her mother's house, took a deep breath, and strode to the door. Never had those damn chimes sounded so ominous. It was she for whom the bells tolled. A white-faced Grace opened the door and pulled her in without a word. She led Andy to the living-room settee, where coffee was waiting, still warm. Cups were poured and sipped. Finally, Andy broke the tense silence.

"Mom, first of all, I'm not suffering from a case of nerves. It didn't start last night, it's something that's been building up for a while now. I must have been bewitched after that romantic week in Stowe. It all happened too fast. It was so different from anything I'd ever known, and, well, Lowell was so attractive. It just seemed magical that he wanted me, good old gawky Andy Ferguson from Denver, Colorado.

"I think I came along just when Lowell was free and looking for something a little different. There I was, an unsophisticated, maybe unspoiled woman with a mind of her own and competitive as hell. He liked that. Then, when I asked him to wait, that must have really triggered him. He can't stand not getting his own way. Then, I think he began to notice how lame I was with his friends. Honestly, Mom, I just felt stupid in all those fancy places. Amy wouldn't, but I do.

"And then he started to talk about my quitting work—that's when it really began to sour. Did you know that he invited Gene Sorley's campaign manager to our party, knowing my feelings about Sorley? It was more than insulting. It hurt. It was just like saying he doesn't take me seriously." Should she mention Vicky? No, no need. Tom? Better not. That would really set Grace off. "So you see, I just can't go through with it."

"I can't believe it. That man is in love with you, Andrea. I'm sure last night was an exception. Now and then, men just have to be men, and we women have to put up with it. I must admit, he seemed rather taken with that model—I don't remember inviting her—Victoria somebody, but's that's just having a last little fling. I bet he's over at your place now with a dozen roses, just waiting to explain."

"No, Mom. Please. I do know him a little better

than you do. He's probably in bed with a terrible hangover, wondering what hit him, but secretly feeling relieved. Anyway, he'd never buy roses. Too ordinary." She almost said, "too expensive," but didn't. "Maybe violets with a quotation from Baudelaire. Very classy."

"Andrea Ferguson! There isn't someone else, is there? Is that what this is all about? Not that candidate you've been writing about, Tom Bradford?"

"Oh, Mom, please. I like Tom a lot. He's really a terrific guy but that's got nothing to do with this. Can't you see it wouldn't work? It was a lovely dream, and I'm so very sorry. Sorry for all of us, especially you, after all you've done for me. I know how much it meant to you. I really do."

Suddenly her mother was weeping and Andy was awkwardly trying to comfort her. They had never been very close, but the thought of hurting her family was hard to bear. She knew how dear to Grace's heart was the thought of being connected to the powerful Curtis family, how it involved her dreams for herself and Amy. Andy had shattered all this. Was she being horribly selfish? No. She was certainly not going to marry to please anyone but herself. She knew Ben would agree— and she knew Ben, wherever he was, was telling her she was right.

Andy and Grace both looked up as they heard the back door slam. Amy always left her bike around the side of the house and sure enough, here she was, pink cheeks and soft blond hair, tangled but pretty.

"Hey, you two. Where's the funeral? What a bash! It was the greatest. And guess what, Ivor Smith asked me to go with him to The Beachcomber tonight. What's the matter, Mom? What's my big sister done now? She tell Lowell where to get off? He was so bombed last night."

"Amy dear, please sit down. As a matter of fact, that's exactly what Andrea has done. I'm afraid I'm still in shock. It doesn't seem possible." Tears threatened again, but Amy was next to her mother hugging her gently in a way Andy had always envied.

"Mommy, don't be upset. Andrea's right. Lowell's okay. He's absolutely gorgeous, but there's something a little creepy about him—the way he danced so close with that Vicky . . . and even me. Ivor says he's always gaga about someone, broken hearts all over Boston. You know something? Andy's too good for him!"

"What?" Grace looked up with surprise. Her face was flushed.

"I mean it, Mom, Andrea has more talent in her little finger than Lowell ever had. So he's good at sailing and tennis and all that, and he's rich. But my sister is going to be one of the best reporters in Boston, in America, in everywhere. Have you read those Tom Bradford articles? They're great. My friend Bill, with the condo, says she's going to get him elected."

"Hey, hold it, Amy!" Andy felt tears of affection spring up. Who would have thought that Amy, little, frivolous Amy, would come to her aid? "I'm not that good yet, but I'm sure gonna try. Oh, Amy, remind me to tell you that I love you. You, too, Mom." The next few minutes were devoted to hugs and eye-dabbing, and a somewhat mollified Grace made her shaky way to the kitchen to make lunch for her girls. She herself announced that she could never eat, but half an hour later she allowed that she might take a little pasta salad and maybe a tiny bloody mary. She felt she deserved it.

But Andy's ordeal was not over. Sure enough, when she returned to Linneaen Street that evening, there was a box with a tiny bouquet of yellow roses and baby's breath sitting outside her front door. A note was attached: *"You're the top, you're the Eiffel Tower ..." Andrea darling, your prince behaved like the frog he sometimes is. Can you ever forgive me? I won't blame you if you don't want to see me for a while but can't we be friends? You're the nicest girl I ever fell for and that's the truth."*

She felt like crying again. It was all too much. It was the roses more than the note itself that wrenched her back to Stowe, to Chez Bernice, and that long-gone night of abandonment in Jason's chalet. Oh, Lowell, it really is a shame things didn't work, she thought, arranging the somewhat wilted buds in her best cream pitcher. She might miss him in the days to come, but right now she was just too tired to think. Thank God tomorrow was Monday. She was going to justify Amy's belief in her. She would show Pete just how good Andy Ferguson could be.

* * *

Andy walked into Pete's office in low heels and a dark blue suit. Very trim and no-nonsense.

"Hi," came the usual gruff salutation. "That was quite a shindig Saturday. That Lowell's a real ladykiller. They were dropping right and left. But no kidding, Andy, you were pretty ruffled that night—and I don't mean the dress. You look great now, though. Have you said anything to your mom?"

"Yeah, boss. It's all right." She would discuss Grace another time. "I hope you've got a really meaty assignment. I'm in the mood for something special. No more parties for a while."

"Glad you said that, Andy. We've had so many letters on the Bradford articles, I've booked you for an hour at his headquarters this morning to get some reaction to the latest polls. Then, and please don't get down and kiss my feet, I'm assigning you the whole campaign, from now until November. Don't say your Uncle Pete doesn't appreciate you. Also, there's something else that's come up. Tell you about it when you get back."

Andy felt the heat in her cheeks. "Pete. Pete, I'm so grateful. Two weeks ago I would have crawled to the state house for that, but now I've got to tell you—I can't."

"Can't!" Pete half-rose in his chair, knocking his cigar out of the ashtray. "What kind of bull am I hearing? Can't? You're not going to quit on me, Andy. I won't let you."

"That's not it, Pete. And you were right about Lowell. He would have wanted me to quit sooner or later. But that doesn't matter anymore." Her voice caught. Next thing she knew, he had her in a big bear hug redolent of cigars and Old Spice. "Take it easy on me, Pete. Breaking the engagement was the hardest thing I've had to do for the past couple of years, but I just had to do it."

"Andy, you're too wise and too real to fall in with that banking crowd. You had me worried. I was afraid you might get tied up with that gang of Sorley backers, but the Bradford stuff was so good, I—"

"That's what I was coming to. There's been a misunderstanding between myself and Mr. Bradford, and I'd rather you sent someone else this morning."

"No way." He released her and began to pace the room. "No way, Andy. What are you talking—misunderstanding? This isn't a Miss Congeniality contest. This is a newspaper. If you had a disagreement, forget it. I've got this interview all lined up for tomorrow's edition. I'll need you back by twelve-thirty so it can be written and sent to the desk by two. I'm counting on you, Andy. Don't let me down."

Did he have to say all that? It was like facing another firing squad. "Okay, Pete," she said tonelessly, "see you at twelve-thirty."

She was glad she had dressed so plainly. She would try to be all reporter. Maybe Tom hadn't seen today's society column and the article on the engagement. She stood tense but determined as she rang the buzzer to his office. The man who greeted her was a far cry from the one who had clasped her hand so tenderly a few short days ago.

"Come in, Ms. Ferguson." She heard the coldness in his voice and shuddered. "I have the questions your editor submitted. We should be able to get through them fairly quickly. Have a seat. Now..."

"Tom," she faltered, "why are you acting like you hardly know me? What's the Ms. Ferguson bit?" She knew they should be professional, but she couldn't bear this icy treatment.

"Do I know you, Ms. Ferguson? Do I know anything at all about you? I thought I did. I thought I'd finally met the woman I've been looking for all these years. Damn it, Andy, I thought you were all the things I wanted—warmth and courage and real compassion, a good head and the talent to use it, never mind being beautiful. But it's all a trick, isn't it? It's a brilliant reporter's trick to break down a guy's defenses, get him all softened up, worm out his intimate secrets for your precious paper, get him to fall head over heels in love with you, then put an end to the job, sign your name, and go back to your real friends."

"Tom, what are you talking about?" She would not cry, she commanded herself. "Tom, I don't know..."

"How do you explain these? Chip showed them to me this morning. Probably guessed how I felt about you."

He handed her the *Trib* society column and a clipping from the *Globe*. There, smiling up at her, was her own face next to Lowell's, taken at the club two weeks ago. Her first impulse was to tear them up, but she simply placed it on the desk with an unsteady hand.

"I didn't want—" She was finding it difficult to speak. "Tom, I should have told you that weekend. I know now. My dad always said to keep my life and work separate, to be a professional, only they started getting mixed up that day on the Cape, and I've been mixed up. Then, the other night at the play they started getting unmixed. I couldn't quite admit it to myself because of all the plans. My poor mom thought I was another Princess Grace or something, but I don't suppose it makes any difference now." Her voice was getting wobbly. "Lowell and I aren't together anymore. I—we're no longer engaged." She thought she had gotten it out rather well. There was a long silence.

"Andy, please don't blame me for asking, but has it got anything to do with me? I meant it about falling in love with you. Good old crusty Tom Bradford—crusading bachelor. Andy, I wanted so much to believe that you were that woman in the theater. When I held your hand, it was like holding all of you. I wanted to give you everything, all of me. I'm not much good at this kind of talk, and I'm not much for fancy restaurants and parties, but I'll change if that's what you—"

"Stop it," she cried, tears blinding her eyes. Then more gently, she whispered, "I'm not like that, not at all. I don't like posh places and glitzy parties. I hate making small talk with people I don't know, and I like hot dogs and tuna fish sandwiches, and I especially like Portuguese soup and brown bread and sea-clam pie." Tears stood in her eyes, but she was grinning her Andy grin. "I like old houses with old-fashioned bathtubs and big old beds, and I love the ocean and—" There was lots more she was going to say but he stopped her with a kiss that made everything clear and right. He held her close, and she ran her hand through his thick, dark hair and down his hard back. They were both trembling.

"Stop now, Tom," she said breathlessly. "We'll have lots of time for that."

"Not enough time in the world," he whispered as he drew back and took a deep, shaky breath. "I'll stop if you promise to see me tonight. And if we get an early start Friday, we can be at Windswept by seven-thirty."

"I promise. Now, Mr. Bradford, if you can spare the time, there are some rather urgent questions I'd like to ask. We've been informed that Gene Sorley has just received the unqualified backing of some of the Cape's most influential banking concerns. This will certainly give his campaign the financial clout it badly needs. How do you intend to counter that?"

ELEVEN

THE NEXT MONTH went by as calmly as a gentle ocean breeze through Windswept. In fact, the weekends at Windswept with Tom were what helped Andy regain a solid footing in her life and work. She loved spending time with him—loved riding, sailing, and just sitting on the big porch, watching the rolling waves and talking for hours. The truth was, she loved *him*. His rugged face, his thick, soft hair, and his Gypsy eyes that darkened when he kissed her. . . .

She smiled with those thoughts as she drove her VW to the *Trib* on a Wednesday morning. She felt so free now, compared to just one month ago. It was as if a heavy weight had been cut from around her neck.

"Hi, Andy. Ready to go to work?" asked Pete as she waltzed into his office.

"You bet I am," said Andy. Pete assigned her four stories. The first amused her to no end.

"I want you to cover the Decorators' Showcase in two weeks. All the top decorators have been assigned to make over a big house in Brookline. They each get a room. See which one you like best."

"Pete, shouldn't the Living Section handle that?"

"I'd rather have a fresh viewpoint. It's yours."

Andy, in a way relieved not to have a pressure story so soon after some recent political coverage, made a mental note to call Amy. Decorating was something Amy knew about even if she refused to take it seriously. They could go together to the house in Brookline and make a day of it. She called Amy and made a date.

"Lunch will be on the *Trib*, Amy. I want you to help me cover the Decorators' Showcase. You know twice as much as I do about ormolu and cachepots."

"I'm flattered," said Amy. "Besides, I have some news for you. I'll tell you when I see you."

That evening, as she and Tom had an after-dinner Scotch on his small terrace, enjoying the lights twinkling on the river and the night air, Andy filled Tom in on what she'd been covering: a suicide pact, a Vietnam reunion, and a picket line in Dorchester. She always wanted to tell him everything, and she wanted to know all about him.

"You always do a thorough job, Andy," he said. "You're really an ace reporter. I'm proud of you. This is going to be a long, hot summer, as you know, but I want to see you as much as possible."

Andy was thrilled, but sensed that he wanted to tell her something. "I want to be with you, too, Tom. You know that," she said. She felt her cheeks redden. She was glad to be hidden by the soft night.

"Well, sweetheart, Sorley has a reputation for dirty tricks. I could care less what he says about me, but he might try to get at you—you know, candidate involved with leading newswoman—that sort of thing. From now on, I think we'd better try to see each other only at Windswept. That place is sacrosanct. I don't let anyone there but you and a few old buddies. Is that all right with you?"

"You know that's my favorite place. That and the ranch. I'll be there whenever we're both free, though I'll be awfully busy this summer, too. In addition to my regular stories I'm going to be covering the campaign of one Tom Bradford."

Two happy weekends at Windswept sped by, and Andy was on the way to her lunch date with Amy. Her sister looked her usual ebullient self. A peach belt cinched her small waist, a pale blue flowered skirt hung in soft folds, and her white linen blouse looked fresh and crisp. Her bare legs and high-heeled blue sandals gave her a jaunty, sexy air. Andy admired her sister, but wished Amy would make something of herself.

"Look at this green chintz, Andy," Amy said as

she headed for the living room of the Decorators' Showcase. "It has a real English country look to it. It's probably a Brunschwig and Fils imitation, but I think it's terrific. Gives the room just that lived-in feeling everybody's looking for."

Andy took notes furiously.

"Amy," said Andy, "you have such a talent with all this. I just wish you'd—"

"Make a career of it?" interrupted Amy. "Well, I might be having other plans. Let's hurry up and finish up the tour, and I'll fill you in on what's trendy and what's out. There's something I want to talk to you about at lunch—or rather someone."

Within an hour, the two sisters were seated in an outdoor café under a yellow-striped umbrella. Andy was eating her usual tuna fish sandwich. Amy toyed with a shrimp salad.

"Andy, I've been seeing someone, and I wanted to talk to you about it. He's really kind of special."

"That's great! Do I know him?"

"You sure do. It's Ivor Smith."

Oh no, thought Andy. Here we go again. The Smiths are just about as snobby as the Curtises. If they didn't come over on the *Mayflower*, it was the next steamer. I'll bet Mom's thrilled. If one daughter can't land a Boston Brahmin, the other will.

"Amy, are you sure you know what you're getting into? Ivor's like Lowell. The same cloth. He'll never wanted you to do anything on your own."

"I'll never be as serious about life as you are, Andy. We have a wonderful time together. He likes me a whole lot. Mom's as pleased as punch. She's counting the minutes until I can go to Shreve's."

"I'm sure she is," laughed Andy. Why couldn't she please her mother the way Amy always did? Daddy would have understood her Lowell decision, but Mom—never.

"There's just one thing that bothers me about my relationship with Ivor," said Amy. "We see each other all the time. He takes me to parties, to The Beachcomber. But some nights he'll get a phone call and be off like a shot. I won't hear from him until the next day, and he'll never tell me where he's been."

"Amy, I'd certainly *ask* him where he's been. Never let anything be swept under the table. How you start is how you finish."

"I've asked him," said Amy, her blue eyes dampening. "He just won't tell me."

"Let me give it some thought." Andy looked at her Timex. "I have to finish up a piece I'm doing on our polluted ocean. Do you know nobody on Cape Cod will eat raw oysters and mussels anymore?"

Amy leaned over the table and squeezed her sister's hand. "Good old Andy. Off and running. You go ahead. I'm going to call Ivor. He should be up by now. It's two o'clock. Call me if you think of anything."

"I will, Amy. And thanks for all your help. I'll knock off the Decorators' Showcase in no time flat."

It was two weeks before Tom could sneak off to meet Andy at Windswept. The campaign was heat-

THE BEST MAN

ing up. Sorley's picture seemed to be everywhere. Visiting a halfway house, his own teenager in hand, opening a newly painted kindergarten in Roxbury, his beaming family surrounding him. Tom was written up, too, his "save our environment" speech made all the national papers, his attack on Sorley's wanting lower taxes on real estate seemed to make a solid impact. But there was no question, thought Andy, a family man made a better visual image than a bachelor, even if the bachelor looked as honest and rugged as Tom. She hoped her last piece on Tom's wanting to shut down a nearby nuclear plant would help. Getting Tom elected, that was what was important.

The blissful weekends were always over too soon. One Sunday night as Tom dropped off Andy, she saw a dark car across Linneaen Street turn on the headlights and take off. Were they waiting for her or was that just her imagination? She decided not to upset Tom, but blew him a kiss good-bye and ran up her steps. The phone, as usual, was ringing.

"Hello . . ."

"Andy, Andy." It was Grace. She was sobbing. "You have to help Amy. Something terrible has happened. Oh, the poor Smiths. You mustn't let them be publicly humiliated. You can save them, and save Amy."

Andy was frightened. Her mother was hysterical. She had never heard her like this. "Slow down, Mom. Now tell me what's happened."

"It's Ivor. You know, Ivor Smith. Well, Amy has

been going out with him. They're practically engaged. Oh, it'd be such a beautiful marriage. They were even talking about Trinity Church and—and then this. He'll never live it down without your help." Andy could hear the deep sobs of her mother.

"What is it, Mom? What's happened?"

"Ivor was picked up last night selling cocaine," she said before sobbing.

"That's terrible, Mom. Where's Amy?"

"She's with Ivor, of course. They're all in seclusion at the Smiths."

"I'll go right over."

"No, dear, that's not what I had in mind."

"What then, Mom? You know I'd do anything to help Amy."

"Good." Grace had suddenly stopped crying. "There was a reporter from the *Tribune* at the house. I want you to make certain this doesn't get in the papers. I'll give a donation to your editor's favorite charity. Anything. The Smiths would be socially ruined if this were printed. You'll see to it. Won't you, dear?" Grace sounded almost wheedling.

Her mother was asking her to compromise herself, her integrity, and that of the *Trib*. Andy knew she could never do this. Her father never would have, nor could she. She just hoped Amy would understand.

"I can't do that, Mom. I can't cover up the news. No reporter would. You know Daddy wouldn't."

"Think of the Smiths; think of Amy," shouted her mother, out of control.

"Mom, think of me," said Andy, softly. She heard the phone click. The peace of Windswept seemed a thousand miles away.

The next few weeks were so hectic Andy had little time to think about Amy, Ivor, or Grace, but her heart ached when she did. A short half-column about Ivor had appeared in the Metro section of the *Trib*. Andy had left messages for Grace, but she had never returned her calls. Amy seemed to have disappeared. Andy saw little of Tom, but they prized the short periods they could snatch for each other all the more.

On a Saturday in August, Pete dispatched her to Plymouth for a Sorley fund-raiser. Tom's campaign had been going well. He was definitely gaining momentum in the polls and running about even with his opponent.

One of the first people she ran into was Lowell, who was conversing with Sorley's campaign manager. Lowell was as charming as ever and insisted on bringing her a vodka and tonic, which she purposely spilled into a nearby azalea bush. Then he introduced her to some banking associates as the hottest little reporter in Boston. "Only watch out," he said, "She's on the other side!" No one seemed to believe him or care. But Lowell really seemed pleased to see her and even complimented her on her white muslin sundress. There was no mention of the past. So like Lowell, she thought. Maybe they could be friends . . . well, at least friendly.

When Sorley rose to make his speech, he beamed like the sun. "I love all my constituents," he said, "even young Bradley, who would undoubtedly regret his misplaced idealism. He wants the government to solve everything. I say, leave it to the boys who know how."

Andy'd heard it all before. She turned back to the refreshment tent, famished as usual, and saw a sinister group of men in dark suits. They were all wearing sunglasses, but she thought she recognized Joey Dyson, a well-known businessman who was rumored to have mob connections. He gave a brief handshake all around and, flanked by two men, walked to a waiting limousine. It was Joey. Now she was certain. It was his slight limp. She had covered a court hearing a year or so before where Joey had been cleared of a bribery charge after a key witness failed to show. Interesting. She might casually mention his name while covering this event and see if it drew fire.

That evening, in a secluded corner of a small bistro in Cambridge, Andy related her adventure to Tom, who consented to meet outside of Windswept. She stopped in midsentence, noticing his frown.

"What is it, Tom?"

"You know, sweetheart, for all his bonhomie, Sorley can be dangerous. This summer is heating up fast, and I don't mean the weather. Let's be very circumspect. If Sorley's gang finds out about us they can easily cry foul. Candidate and columnist in collusion—or worse."

He leaned back and looked at Andy, who was twisting a curl around her finger in thought. "Oh,

THE BEST MAN

I'm probably being overprotective of us," he said. "I look forward to our weekends so."

Andy, understanding as always, squeezed his hand. "Okay, I've got a wild week anyway. But come next weekend, it's Windswept for us."

Andy arrived at the office early the next day. A bedraggled, blond figure was huddled in the club chair by her desk. Andy realized with a start that it was Amy. Andy felt a knot in her stomach. She knew Amy must have suffered a good deal because of Ivor. She wished she hadn't felt obligated to allow the story to be printed. Sometimes being a reporter was a rotten business.

Amy looked up. She had no makeup on. Her skin was blotchy, her eyes bloodshot and swollen with dark circles underneath.

"Andy," she said, "I just want you to know I respect you for printing the story about Ivor, hard as it's been for me to take. I—I think I might love Ivor, but I need some time now. I'll stick by him, but it's high time I try to make something of myself. Singing the night away in The Beachcomber just isn't enough. I want to go to a first-rate design school and be a topnotch decorator. I don't know if I have what it takes, but I can surely try." She put her head between her hands, and Andy could hear muffled sobs.

"Amy, Ivor's a lucky guy to have you. Maybe he can put all this behind him and be the stronger for it. If he loves you, he'll support your decision. I'm proud of you, Amy."

"Thanks, Andrea. It's the hardest decision I've

ever had to make. Maybe I'll be losing Ivor, but then—like you say—if so, he isn't worth it."

"Right on, Amy," said Andy, and then in a wistful voice added, "I wish Mom were as mature as you've been. We never saw eye to eye, Amy, but I miss her all the same. I want her to share my happiness."

"I can't speak for Mom," said Amy, her blue eyes now beginning to shine, "but you're the best sister anybody could have. Come on, I'll buy you a cup of coffee."

On the following Tuesday, the *South Shore Times*, a small newspaper controlled by Sorley, carried the headline, TRIBUNE REPORTER AND BRADFORD COZY TWOSOME.

Pete called Andy into his office and, grim-faced, handed her the copy. She read it quickly and stared back at him, angry and bewildered.

"We were so careful, Pete. We hardly ever met in Boston, only on the Cape, because he was afraid of something like this. Oh, my God, they must have followed us. They know abut Windswept, even the names of restaurants and beaches. It's so degrading."

"It's worse than that, Andy. It's a blow to the *Trib*. This could be picked up by all the competition. We'll be accused of slanted journalism, conflict of interest. You know we've always been proud of our objectivity. We don't print facts until we're sure of them. You're off the campaign, as of now. I don't know what we can do to repair bridges except to make an announcement that you are on a well-deserved vacation and Gabriel Tilson will continue the election coverage."

"But, Pete, that's as good as saying they're telling the truth."

"Aren't they?"

Andy fought back tears.

"Pete, it all happened a short time ago. You know I was all set to marry Lowell. I thought I loved him and then I met Tom. I knew he was the man I really wanted. Don't you see? The reason I fell in love with him is because all those things I wrote about him were the truth. That's who he is. Remember? I asked you to take me off the story and you wouldn't." She blew her nose loudly.

"Come here, kid," said Pete, drawing a chair next to him and circling her trembling shoulders with his broad arm. "I guess I was a little blind and maybe you weren't exactly candid with me."

"How could I be? I was sure he'd hate me when he found out about Lowell. The day you made me go over there was the day we both knew how much we needed each other. Since that assignment, I haven't written a word about him. Have I?"

"Not about him. That's true. Hmmm. Then, that's the way we'll play it. You write a short piece in your column stating why you can no longer continue reporting on Bradford. Truth is best. There may be some repercussions, but we may even get some converts. All the world loves a lover."

Andy wrenched herself away. "If I didn't love

you so much, I'd punch you. That's as bad as those celebrity tabloids. Making copy out of personalities. I feel like I'm walking through garbage. I feel like changing my name and going to Outer Mongolia. Meanwhile, I'm going home and resign from the whole rat race."

"Andy! Wait—"

But she was gone. Back in her apartment, she felt drained and somehow still dirty after a long shower. For a long time she sat staring at nothing, lost and desolate. Finally, after much tormented thought, she wrote:

Darling Tom,

By now you will have seen the filth in the South Shore Times. *No doubt other papers will follow. I feel that without meaning to, I've hurt you more than anyone. We should have known better than to think we could love each other openly, even in Truro.*

You were so right about Sorley. I dropped that hint in my column about Dyson's being at that rally and they dropped their own bomb. I know they won't let up. Not till one of you wins and you, my love, are going to win despite all their money and innuendos. But without me. I've thought and thought and there's only one way to go.

Tomorrow, I'll announce my leave of absence from the Trib *and here's the hardest part. I can't see you anymore. Maybe, when all of this is over—Tom, I tried not to fall in love with you, keep the job separate, all of that, but I did and now I've hurt your chances. Not just you, but all the people counting on you to beat the Sorleys who talk big and do nothing to make things better, as you surely will.*

I'm trying to make things better by getting out of your life now.

Andy

She ached all over. Her head hurt. She couldn't sleep. She finally dozed off only to awake four hours later feeling tired but much calmer. She would be late! Oh, no. It didn't matter now. She made coffee and realized how ravenous she was. After wolfing down eggs and toast she began to feel almost alive. She reread the letter without flinching and sealed it, stamped it, and mailed it hurriedly on her way to the *Tribune*.

She was halfway to Pete's office when he peered out and motioned her to come in.

"I think we're in luck. I've got just the tonic you need. No more Bradford for you, agreed, but that lead you got on Sorley and Dyson may be about to erupt in our favor. We just got a call from an informant about a bad job of arson on Dyson's business rivals last night. The informant says he's got evidence that it was a Dyson job. Let's hope the Dyson story will put that gossip stuff on the back burner. Meanwhile, you take a short leave of absence."

That week the D.A.'s office followed a trail of payoff money from Dyson's accounts, some of which had landed in Sorley's campaign coffers. The indignant candidate disclaimed any knowledge it. He immediately offered to renounce any such contributions and threatened, "Heads will roll!" He then made an impassioned speech about the cancer of organized crime.

Andy, now on her leave of absence, avoided her apartment. And when there, she refused to answer the telephone. Her one satisfaction was her realization of how fortunate she was to have broken with Lowell before making an irreversible mistake. Her whole infatuation seemed so trivial now. What had that been, compared to the knowledge of her fierce love for Tom? It was there, tearing at her heart, but she would not compromise him again. Maybe there was a future. Or maybe it was too late. . . .

On a Sunday, almost ten days after her confrontation with Pete, she ran downstairs in her sweat pants to jog around the Charles and found a haggard Tom Bradford waiting outside her apartment building. She started to turn back. But the next moment, she felt his arms around her, and the solid ice of her resolve melted in his embrace.

"Andy, my darling Andy. I've been calling and calling. They were holding my personal mail in Truro. I didn't know until yesterday. I read that piece about us in that South Shore rag. I was afraid you'd be hurt. I called the *Trib* and all they could say was that you were on leave and couldn't be reached. I kept waiting to hear from you. I finally got hold of your mother, and she said you'd had some kind of blowup and that you hadn't spoken for a time. I was worried sick. I got here as fast as I could."

"Oh, Tom. Can't you see how bad this could be for you?"

"I can see how bad it's already been for you, sweetheart. There is a perfectly simple solution, you know: You can marry me! We can put the announcement in the *Trib* this week. Will you, Andy Ferguson, be my wife? Say yes. Damn it, you know you're the only woman for me—now and forever. Will you, Andy? Say it now . . ."

At that moment, two blue-jeaned students with book bags turned to see a tall woman in green sweat pants wildly hugging a rather attractive man with dark, tousled hair. He seemed quite nonresistant.

At ten o'clock the evening of the election, an ungracious Gene Sorley conceded defeat. A shout of joy went up in Truro's Masonic Hall. Tom made a short speech. He thanked the people of the Lower Cape ending with, "Friends, I'd like you to meet my wife-to-be, Ms. Andy Ferguson."

A tremendous roar went up, and Andy stepped forward to take Tom's hand and wave to the delighted crowd.

Afterward Tom and Andy drove back to Windswept to savor their mutual triumph alone, in the quiet of the lovely old house. Shoes off, in front of a crackling fire, the first of the season, they snuggled back in a pleasant weariness.

"Tom, I'm so happy. I figure my dad is smiling, too. And, Tom, thank you for teaching me what it's like to be really in love."

TWELVE

Andy turned off Route 6 onto the Pamet River Road. It was twilight. The December air was brisk. She was glad to be wearing Tom's torn fishermen's sweater because the heater in her VW had stopped for good long ago.

I must have that repaired, she thought. I will. When I have time. Andy laughed to herself. So when will I have time? Not with my career, not with Tom, who'll be spending time in Washington. Yes. We have a whole lifetime to build together, but the heater will have to be put on hold. Right now it was just one day until the wedding of Tom Bradford and Andy Ferguson!

"You take Friday off," Pete said. "That ought to give you two lovebirds plenty of time to get ready."

"Just remember, Pete. The wedding's Saturday at four-thirty. Be sure to leave your desk by one. That ought to give you plenty of time to get there. And don't forget to have your blue suit cleaned."

"I won't misbehave, Andy. Not until afterward," said Pete. "Oh, in case I don't have time to tell you later," he said, and Andy saw him blush for the first and last time, "Tom Bradford's a damn lucky guy."

A slight chill came over Andy as she thought of The Ritz and all those old aborted plans for the Trinity Church affair. How could anything that was so wrong have ever seemed so right? Two hundred and fifty Boston Brahmins had to find something else to do that June twentieth. Goodbye forever to Lowell Curtis, The Beachcomber, The Somerset, Trinity Church, Beacon Hill, and Cambridge Tennis Club. And hello, Tom Bradford, campaigns, deadlines, late-night phone calls, and chaos! This will be your life, Andy Ferguson. Hooray!

Andy couldn't wait to see Tom. As she drove down the winding road to the ocean and Windswept, she noticed that the small farmhouses along the way were all lit up. Wreaths were on every door and Christmas lights shone from within. There was a ring around the full moon. Oh well, a misty wedding day would be just fine. The familiar locusts had shed their leaves long ago, but occasional holly trees and bushes were bright with red berries. No cars were buzzing back and forth to the beach, no families weighted with

THE BEST MAN 231

towels and coolers. Truro was remote, it was still, it beckoned her to her destiny.

Windswept was aglow, candles in every window. Tom was there to greet her. In his blue jeans, red plaid flannel shirt, and heavy boots he looked better than ever. He enveloped Andy in his strong arms and, hand in hand, they went into the large country kitchen. "There's a thick Portuguese soup simmering on the stove," he said. "Lots of *linguica*, beans and kale. It'll warm the cockles of your heart."

"Just seeing you does that," said Andy. Everything with Tom was so natural. Just like it should be. Just right.

"How about a Scotch on the rocks for a weary traveler, Congressman Bradford?" she said.

"Sold," said Tom.

They sat at the dented pine kitchen table as Andy told Tom about Amy.

"You know, Tom, she's turned out to be true blue, a Ferguson through and through. It still surprises me that she understood exactly why I had to print the whole story about Ivor. It took real guts, but she's got her head on straight, at last. She's doing well at that design school in New York City. She'll knock the Big Apple on its ear. I'm so proud of her. I—I just wish Mom would come around. Why must she be so stubborn?"

"Hmmph," said Tom. "Always wondered where you got that stubborn streak. Someday she'll understand you did what you had to. Now listen, Ms. Ferguson, tomorrow is our wedding day, and we've never even discussed the guest list. You said

I should invite who I wanted, so I asked the neighbors on Pamet River Road, and a few guys from Boston. I don't know who'll show up, but I guarantee you my staff won't miss this."

"Pete's the one I'm worried about. I told him the wedding was at four-thirty Saturday and that he had to be on time. After all, he's giving me away."

"I'm glad you decided to have Pete do that," said Tom as he cut himself a chunk of Vermont cheese. "Your father would be pleased."

Andy decided, for about the one hundredth time that week, that she was about the luckiest person in Massachusetts.

"Mrs. Souza is concocting her special wedding cake doused with rum, and two friends of mine are going to bring in enough oysters to feed a fleet," said Tom. "I guess I'll be pretty busy shucking. Speaking of which, I just happen to have a few samples in the fridge for my fair lady. How about it?"

"Oysters, Portuguese soup, and you. An unbeatable trio," said Andy as Tom produced a bowlful of the mollusks and an oyster knife. Andy, never one to let events interfere with her appetite, ate heartily.

Tom stood up and held Andy close to him. He kissed her mouth, her eyes, her hair. "Why don't you go try on my grandmother's wedding dress one last time?" he said. "I put it in the steamer trunk in the guest room for safekeeping."

Andy left the kitchen and walked through the living room. Tom had put garlands of pine on the mantel, where two pewter vases filled with holly stood on either side of his mother's tall candlesticks. The pine floor creaked under the hooked rugs. Andy felt at home here. Close to Tom and, in a new way, nearer to her father than she had been in a long time. She knew Tom would feel the same way about the ranch and loved him all the more for having agreed to spend their honeymoon there.

She climbed the stairs and entered the guest room. A heavy, carved maple double bed took up almost all of the space. At the foot of the bed was the steamer trunk. The same kind, she was certain, that her Grandmother Littleton had probably owned. Andy lifted the lid, and there, wrapped in yellowed tissue paper, was Tom's grandmother's dress. Andy held it up. It was simple. White lawn with a high neck. Long sleeves with cuffs of lace. Gathered at the waist, the skirt fell in gentle folds to the floor. There was a small train. Andy pulled off her jeans and fisherman's sweater and slipped into the dress. Her trim waist looked even smaller, the long skirt fell gently over her slim hips.

"You look spectacular. It's as if the dress were made for you," said Tom. His voice startled her. She wheeled around and in doing so, tripped on the train and fell into his arms. But not before she heard a terrifying sound. The delicate cotton was ripping. She looked down. Her knee protruded.

"Tom, oh, Tom, I've ruined everything. How can I march down the aisle of that beautiful church with my knee sticking out of your grandmother's dress?"

"That's my Andy," said Tom.

"Tom, stop teasing," said Andy. "What can we do? I'm no good with my hands except at a word processor."

Tom produced a Swiss army knife.

"No way, Congressman Bradford. Don't touch this dress. I'll just worry about it later."

"Okay, Andy love, to bed, to bed. Just one more night before we're joined forever."

"I can't wait for tomorrow," she said. "It's going to be a perfect wedding. If only Daddy could have met you. If only Mom would come..."

By the next morning a fog had settled over Truro. Andy could see nothing when she peeked out of the kitchen window. The only sound was that of Tom's chopping logs for the living room and kitchen fireplaces. Then Andy heard the sound of a car coming up the long, winding dirt driveway and then Tom's voice.

"Hi, Mrs. Souza. I'd recognize the roar of your pickup truck anywhere. You're sure out early."

"You know all about early birds, Tom Bradford."

"Andy," shouted Tom. "Here's Mrs. Souza with our wedding dinner!"

Andy ran out and peeped in the back of the pickup truck stacked with loaves of Portuguese bread, cheeses, and steak-and-kidney pies. She couldn't help thinking of the Perfect Palate Caterers and their pink van. Mrs. Souza, her flannel skirt covered with a butcher's apron, was a far cry from the starched black-and-white uniforms.

As Andy brought in the first load of Portuguese bread, she heard the phone ringing. First crisis of the day, thought Andy as she picked up the receiver. It was Amy.

"Hi, Andrea. I just got to Winthrop House. It took me four hours from Newton. This weather's a real pea souper."

Andy hoped Pete would leave in plenty of time. Even Saturdays, when he put the *Trib* to bed, he checked over the major copy for problems or errors.

"I know you and Tom are doing everything yourselves," said Amy, "but I wondered if you needed some help decorating the church. I'm pretty good at that, you know."

Andy was touched. Amy had turned out to be the greatest sister. And she was going to be a wonderful decorator. She had finally broken up with Ivor, but Andy was certain that she'd soon find someone who complemented her just the way Andy had. After all, it had taken twenty-six years for Andy to get her own act together.

"Amy, that'd be super. I'll grab some scissors and clippers, and we'll go cut some holly and pine. Put on some warm pants. I'll be right over."

Andy hung up, but the phone started ringing again.

"Hi, is Tom Bradford there? This is Tippy Kahn. I just wanted a few details for the *Cape Codder* of the wedding this afternoon. We've got it scheduled for front-page news."

"Maybe I can help you. I'm Andy Ferguson."

"Oh, of course. I've read your column and lead

stories often in the *Trib*, Ms. Ferguson. I'm sure you can tell me anything we'd like to know," said Tippy.

This is how it's going to be from now on, thought Andy. Tom will always be front-page news. At least I hope so. She filled Tippy in on the details and then asked him, "Why don't you come cover the wedding yourself? We'd both like to have you here. . . . Fine, see you then."

"I heard that invitation," said Tom as he kicked the kitchen door open, his arms full of wood. "You're a born politician's wife."

"Nope, I'm a born reporter who's also going to be a politician's wife, which I'll fill you in on later. Right now, Amy and I are going to decorate the church." said Andy.

"Nothing too fancy, ma'am," said Tom.

"Don't worry. Just practice those wedding vows you're going to surprise me with. See ya later."

Andy blew Tom a kiss and sped to the Winthrop House in her VW. Amy was waiting outside in ski pants and hiking boots. "Hi, Andrea, look at me. I'm going native."

"I'm really glad to see you, Amy. We have to hurry. We have to cut pine branches and holly leaves and—"

"Hold it," said Amy. "I haven't been your sister for all these years without learning something." She reached into a white canvas L.L. Bean bag and produced red and white satin ribbons, wire threads, candles, and candle holders. "I knew you'd say, 'I don't have any time,' so I just brought these things with me from New York."

"Amy Ferguson, you could be a wedding planner, a—"

"Come on, big sis," said Amy. Andy noticed Amy was looking at her in a resigned and tolerant way. They drove to the Pamet River. It was low tide and the two sisters, one blond and bouncy, the other dark and lithe, walked along the bank picking branches of wild berries and evergreens. The fog had not lifted, but it didn't seem to matter to them.

"Look at that beautiful holly tree," said Andy.

"Nobody will miss a few branches," said Amy as she snipped off a few choice ones. "Even your beloved Tom can't say I've totally destroyed the ecology."

The back of the tiny car was soon filled, and the two women drove around the river and up Cemetery Road to Fisher Lane. There, at the end of the lane, high on a hill, and hidden from view except for the enormous white steeple that could be seen from the bay to the ocean, was the Truro Congregational Church. Built in 1806, it was the oldest church in the area. To Andy it represented a beautiful simplicity, a purity—an honesty of spirit that she also found in Tom.

"Come on," said Amy. "Let's go in."

Andy opened the door. In the front, high up, was the pulpit. The seats of the tiny church were padded in a frayed red velvet. Amy got right to work. She tied branches, evergreens, and holly together with big red and white satin bows and wired the arrangements to the end of each pew. Inside each, she stapled a candle. She tacked an enormous bouquet on the front of the pulpit. Andy stood and watched in amazement.

"Amy, you're a whiz," she said.

"Just wait till I have my designer's degree," said Amy. "I'm chomping at the bit to finish school and start working."

Andy gave Amy a big hug. She was going to be okay. Andy knew it. She'd find her way just as Andy had. Never mind that it would be in a different direction. She looked at her Timex—twelve o'clock. Pete would be leaving the *Trib* in an hour. And the fog showed no sign of lifting.

Andy tore back to Windswept. Only two hours to show time, she thought. What a lucky duck I am, she thought as she went over and hugged Tom, who was on the phone.

"Hi, Pete," Tom was saying. "You're where? Falmouth? Oh, my God, you took the wrong turn when you got off the Sagamore Bridge. What? I know it's hard to see the signs in this fog."

Pete. In Falmouth! He'd never make it, thought Andy.

"Pete, you just get back on Route Six and head straight down the Cape," said Tom. "I'll have someone meet you at the Truro turnoff. He'll take you right to the church. You ought to just about make it. Hurry up now. You're part of the cast of characters."

Andy pulled off her slicker and heavy boots. She showered quickly and then pulled the delicate wedding dress over her shoulders. It fit like a glove. She turned to look at herself in the mirror. Horrified, she noticed the rip she had forgotten to

THE BEST MAN 239

repair. "Help," she wailed. "Emergency, emergency." There was a knock on the door.

"Tom, come in, for heaven's sakes. It's crisis city in here."

The door opened, ever so slowly. There, in a green velvet Empire dress, gold high heels, hair impeccably coiffed, stood Grace. "Andrea," she said tearfully, "may I come in?"

Andy, her soft, gray eyes moist, rushed to her mother, tearing her dress more as she ran—but that didn't matter now.

"Mom, Mom, I—I can't believe it. This is the best wedding present I could ever have."

"Andy. I'm so sorry. Will you ever forgive me? I've been selfish, so concerned with what people would think, Amy involved with a—a dope peddler. Now I've said it. That's what Ivor was. You were right, of course. You had to print the story ... do your job. That's what your father would have done. I—I guess I've had to do a lot of growing up fast. It was a long time coming. Will you ever forgive me?"

"It's over, Mom. It's over. Now," she grinned her Andy grin. "Hey, how about grabbing some pins and helping me out?"

Together, the two of them, through their happy tears, quickly pinned up Andy's wedding dress.

"Andrea, you look beautiful. I'm proud to be your mother. I—I just wish Ben were here to see you."

"Me, too, Mom. But I'm just glad you are."

As the three of them—Andy, Tom, and Grace—drove from Windswept to the Truro Congregational Church, Andy looked back at the eccentric, handsome old house that had meant so much to Tom, and that she had grown to love as she had grown to love its owner. No matter what went wrong, she'd have Tom at Windswept from now on. And when they next returned there, she and Tom would be husband and wife—together for now and forever. . . .

The minister was standing in the pulpit in a dark suit and a bright red tie. The small church was filled with people, and candlelight bathed the walls. The long, arched windows reflected the bright ribbons and fresh greens. It was 4:25. Where was Pete? The guests, conducted by Reverend Metzger, sang, "O, Little Town of Bethlehem" and "Hark, the Herald Angels Sing." It was 4:29. Suddenly Andy heard the roar of a car motor. Pete, rumpled trenchcoat over his shiny blue suit, tie askew, ran to the entrance.

"Hi, kid. You know I'd never miss a deadline." Pete handed his trenchcoat to Jim, and, as everyone sang "Deck the Halls with Boughs of Holly," Pete took Andy by the arm and down the aisle to where Tom awaited her.

"Friends of Andrea and Thomas," said Reverend Metzger. "We have come here to celebrate the marriage of two very special people. The Bradfords have been here for generations. Whalers, people of the sea.

"Tom Bradford is a pilgrim, a fair man we are proud to have represent us. Andrea Ferguson, too, is a pioneer. She comes to Truro from Colorado, from the Rockies. Here, in this tiny church where the two of them have decided to join together, the mountains meet the sea. They are individualists, our bride and groom. They wish to say their own vows. Andrea..."

Andy stood tall, took Tom's hand, and looked into his dark eyes as she said in a loud, firm voice: "Each time a man stands up for an ideal, or acts to improve the lot of others, he sends a tiny ripple of hope. And when at some future date the high court of history sits in judgment of each of us, our success or failure, in whatever office we hold, will be measured by the answers to four questions: First, were we truly courageous? Second, were we truly wise? Third, were we truly good? Finally, were we truly dedicated? In you, Tom Bradford, I have found all these things. And one more—a capacity for love that truly inspires me. And so I promise my own love and honor to you for all time."

Tom grasped Andy's hand. They stood in the December twilight, and as Tom began his vows, the fog lifted and the late-afternoon sun lit the church:

Time and again I've longed for adventure/
Something to make my heart beat the faster/
What did I long for? I never really knew/
Finding your love I found my venture/
Touching your hand my heart beats the faster/
All that I want in this world is you.

Reverend Metzger whispered to Andy and Tom. "The rings, children, the rings."

Tom placed the gold band on Andy's tapered finger. "With this ring I wed you, Andy Ferguson. I give you all my love and we will go through life together as equal partners."

Then Andy took Tom's left hand. "I marry you, Tom Bradford, knowing we will share all the joys and pain our life will bring us. Fulfilled in the knowledge that through our mutual strength and love no obstacle will be too great."

"And now," said Reverend Metzger, "Andrea Littleton Ferguson and Thomas Bradford, I pronounce you husband and wife."

Tom let go of Andy's hands and, arms outstretched, he reached to take his beloved in his arms and give her their first married kiss. As Andy stepped forward, she heard, in the silence of that moment, a pin drop. No, several pins. She looked down to see the rip had opened again in her dress. Knees showing, she gazed at her husband, horrified. Tom, without a moment's hesitation, swept her in his arms, and, as Reverend Metzger led their friends in "It Came Upon A Midnight Clear," Tom Bradford carried his new bride out of the church. Once in the car, Andy and Tom burst out laughing, then gazed at each other and sighed with immense pleasure.

"Looks like we might have some overnight guests," said Tom. "They're predicting snow."

"Fine with me," said his new bride. "Come on. Let the festivities begin! But, Tom, darling Tom, can I get out of this dress?"

"You can wear a bikini if you like, Mrs. Bradford. And I promise not to call you that anywhere but at home."

"No, I like it. Isn't that funny? I like it. Mrs. Tom Bradford. Lovely. Andy Ferguson at work. Mrs. Bradford at Windswept."

The wedding party assembled inside the kitchen, where a big bowl of glug had just been poured.

"That's my version of mulled wine. I throw in raisins and currants for flavor and plenty of brandy. Help yourselves, everybody," shouted Tom above the din.

Andy thought the house had never looked so fine, so welcoming. The fire and candles and tiny lights on the tree lent their special enchantment.

The wedding party was crowding into the living room, having dined heartily on oysters and steak-and-kidney pie. Tom rose and said, "I would like to make a toast to the beautiful bright woman who was brave enough to believe in me from the first and even braver to marry me. To Andy!"

"To Tom," she said, rising, "who will always be the man for me."

A light snow had begun to fall, softly, silently. Andy's cheeks glowed as she joined Tom and the wedding guests in "God Bless the Master of this House," followed by "Good King Wenceslas," which was Tom's favorite. He was the only one who knew all the words, and his ragged baritone did most of the work.

A little later, a sleepy Andy looked at Tom meaningfully and the two rose to say good night.

"There's plenty of drink and grub, lots of wood," said Tom. "Help yourselves to everything."

The stairs were chilly, but Tom had lit the fire in the master bedroom. In silent communication, they both paused before entering. Tom slipped his arms around his bride, and Andy turned to her new husband, resting her hands on his strong shoulders.

"The marriage bed awaits," he murmured.

"I'm glad," she teased. "It's too cold to sleep alone." Smiling, she moved her fingers in a gentle massage, then delighted in watching his eyes darken. " 'For I'd rather one kiss from the Gypsy's lips/Than all of your land and money oh/Than all of your land and money oh. . . . ' That song always reminded me of you—my dark-eyed Gypsy."

Tom pulled her closer and with a husky whisper asked, "How did I get so lucky?"

"I'm the lucky one, my love. . . . "

Gently, he brushed a kiss to her forehead, then in one swift motion, she was in his arms.

"Tom!" she exclaimed in surprise, clinging to his sturdy body for balance.

"Time for bed," he said simply before moving toward the flickering light of their warm bedroom and kicking the door shut behind him.

She laughed with sheer joy when he carried her inside, knowing they were moving together across a threshold and toward a life of love that was only just beginning.

Watch for OTHERWISE ENGAGED,
the next BRIDE AND GROOM *romance
coming to you soon from Lynx Books:*

OTHERWISE ENGAGED

Anya Kayne and Peter Siler love each other, but they both work in a company that frowns upon inter—office romance. After a year of tiptoeing around the office—and turning down colleagues who're always trying to arrange blind dates—Peter decides to go public. He wants stability in his life and he loves Anya, so he proposes.

Anya is enthusiastic about the engagement, but along with Peter's proposal, she accepts an offer to join the staff of a newspaper and fulfills a dream of becoming a journalist. Her demanding new career leaves practically no time for Peter, or to help plan the large formal wedding that Peter insisted upon and Anya was never crazy about in the first place.

Anya adores Peter, but she wants to succeed in her career; and Peter cherishes Anya, but he won't settle for less than a full commitment. Frustrated, confused, and harried, Peter and Anya both admit that they like the idea of a *wedding*, but they wonder . . . After the vows are said, the bouquet is thrown, and the last bite of cake is eaten, will their love survive a modern *marriage*?

About the Author:

Robin St. Joan is a freelance journalist and a part-time resident of Cape Cod, Massachusetts. This is her first novel.